MURDER
CAN BE
RELATIVE

To Jim
Best Wishes
Lila
Jan/95

Hope you enjoy this
book at least as much as
we enjoyed the beet borscht.
Ha! Ha! All my best.
Lucy.

MURDER
CAN BE
RELATIVE

LILA L. PHILLIPS

Northwest Publishing Inc.
Salt Lake City, Utah

Murder Can Be Relative

All rights reserved.
Copyright © 1994 Lila L. Phillips

Reproductions in any manner, in whole or in part,
in English or in other languages, or otherwise
without written permission of the publisher is prohibited.

This is a work of fiction.
All characters and events portrayed in this book are fictional,
and any resemblance to real people or incidents is purely coincidental.

For information address: Northwest Publishing, Inc.
6906 South 300 West, Salt Lake City, Utah 84047
JC 06 06 94

PRINTING HISTORY
First Printing 1994

ISBN: 1-56901-218-0

NPI books are published by Northwest Publishing, Incorporated,
6906 South 300 West, Salt Lake City, Utah 84047.
The name "NPI" and the "NPI" logo are trademarks belonging to
Northwest Publishing, Incorporated.

PRINTED IN THE UNITED STATES OF AMERICA.
10 9 8 7 6 5 4 3 2 1

Murder Can Be Relative is dedicated to the memory of my father (Papa), whose belief in me encouraged me to believe in myself.

Acknowledgments

To my husband, Mike Kilburn, who prompted me to start writing, and wouldn't take no for an answer. Thank you for the inspiration and the love.

To my family, whom I love dearly.

Last, but definitely not least, to the nurses and doctors (past and present) of the Coronary Care Unit at Colchester Regional Hospital, Truro, Nova Scotia, who have had the good grace to put up with me for the last fifteen years. There simply does not exist a finer group of people.

1

Melissa could not believe her good fortune. Her aunt was embarking on a Caribbean cruise and, due to her doctor's insistence that she be accompanied by a qualified nurse, Judith had chosen her niece to be her delegated companion. The combination of Melissa's ten years of cardiac nursing experience, blended with Judith's fondness for her niece, made Melissa the most logical candidate.

Her aunt's call had come as Melissa was preparing for a twelve-hour night shift. The nurse preferred these hours of duty for several reasons, not the least of which being the opportunity to escape the general state of confusion which was part and parcel of working during the day. Freedom was also a much appreciated ingredient associated with working at a time when most of the patients were sleeping and, generally, managerial staff was off duty. There were few authoritative individuals to answer to, and the innumerable phone calls one received during daylight hours became virtually nonexistent after midnight.

With the absence of many of the day shift duties, Melissa used this time to best advantage. She spent countless hours conversing with her clients and responding to their questions. By doing so, she was able to allay many of the fears which tend to preoccupy a person's mind during a hospital stay. Melissa had discovered, by virtue of these impromptu chats, that the change in personality mentioned by friends and family, was merely a means by which the hospitalized individual asserted what little independence they retained, once entering hospital doors. If they became difficult to deal with, usually, it was an expression of fear mingled with frustration over the need to accept the fact that they were no longer in control of their own affairs. Decisions in this regard were now in the hands of total strangers. Strangers who were not always of the friendly variety.

Scheduling meal times, the appropriate time to bathe and, on occasion, the hour to retire was no longer under their jurisdiction. Control over the daily activities of one's existence is, to many, extremely difficult to relinquish. If more health care workers were exposed to the other side of the medical profession, Melissa felt quite certain they would be better able to appreciate the absolute terror involved with the hospitalization experience.

Judith's suggestion came at a most opportune time, as Mel was presently in a quandary as to how, and when, she planned to spend her annual leave. Postings were due at the hospital early, a common source of irritation for employees. It was difficult to decide, in March, the preferred interval one wished to select for vacation. The deadline was essential, management explained, to ensure that all employees received their entitled leave, while guaranteeing adequate staffing coverage. As the available relief staff for specialized units, such as

C.C.U., did not comprise a long list, it was imperative that vacations be scheduled early.

"Dear," pleaded Judith, "you really must agree to accompany me. My heart is set on cruising and I cannot think of a single soul I would rather travel with. You know how stubborn Dr. Adams can be. He fears I will lose control of my wheelchair and fall overboard or, at the very least, neglect to take my medication as prescribed. Since he is familiar with your credentials, through your affiliation with the hospital, he is agreeable to the excursion, if you are present to ensure my well-being."

"How could I possibly refuse such a generous offer? Will Suzanne and Donald be going on the cruise as well?"

"No, they have no desire to be saddled with an invalid mother. They feel their activities would be somewhat curtailed if they were responsible for watching out for me. Either of my less than doting offspring, I fear, would not hesitate in helping me over the ship's edge, or be adverse to giving me the wrong dosage of medication."

"Aunt Judith, surely you are mistaken!" Melissa, though not overly fond of her cousins, found it difficult to believe they would, in any way, harm their mother.

"There is a lot of money involved, Melissa. You never know what a person is capable of doing, especially when the outcome is independent wealth. My children have grown accustomed to a certain lifestyle which, when one reaches maturity, becomes more costly to maintain. They have always resented deeply the idea of receiving a monthly allowance, preferring to be awarded their trust fund in one lump sum. Upon my death, the money would be theirs without restriction.

"The only reason I made the present arrangement with my lawyer, in regard to the delving out of funds, is due to their ineptitude with finances, a weakness inherited from their father. My husband, however, had enough positive attributes to overshadow that one glaring fault. Attributes which, unfortunately, were not transferred in his genes. Because of those other positive traits, I never had the heart to tell him it was I who salvaged the business when his excessive spending brought us, on more than one occasion, to the brink of financial ruin."

"Mother and I always suspected that to be the case," admitted Mel. "Uncle Howard was an extraordinary man in many ways, though 'financial wizard' was not a title he could lay claim to. I'm certain he was aware of your efforts and knew that your love for him was what kept you silent. On the other hand, his intense adoration for you, no doubt, prevented him from revealing such insight. It is not surprising that your marriage was so successful."

"Enough of this sentiment," Judith remarked, her voice thick with emotion. "Will you accompany me, or not?" As usual, Judith tried to appear gruff when she wished to disguise her true feelings.

"I would be delighted to do so. When is the date of your departure?"

"A month from today. I realize that doesn't allow you much time to prepare. However, in anticipation of your positive response, I have already purchased the tickets. Arrangements have been made, barring your refusal, to release you from active hospital duty for the month we will be away. They will not require you to use vacation time. Instead, they suggested denoting it as a tour of private duty. You will be paid your normal salary, the only difference being that I will pay you for your services."

"That is not necessary, Judith. I am more than willing to use my annual leave, as I have no definite plans for it anyway."

"Nonsense, this will be a working vacation. Besides, if you were unable to go, I would have to pay a regular private duty nurse. I insist on making this arrangement and, as you are aware, I always get my way." Judith chuckled with this statement, even though both ladies knew that, essentially, it was true.

"Okay. Far be it from me to refuse such an exciting offer. See you in a month."

"I will be in touch, in a couple of weeks, to finalize details. Till then, take care."

The ladies said their good-byes.

Concentration became the major obstacle for Melissa during the subsequent weeks. With the prospect of such a delightful journey preoccupying her thoughts, it was exceedingly difficult to concentrate on mundane obligations, such as nursing duties and her day-to-day responsibilities.

To say Mel's peers were a trifle envious was an understatement. The very idea of being paid to travel on a cruise was unbelievable, to say the least. Although, by definition, it would be a working holiday, it was apparent that the nursing aspect of the trip was sure to be kept to a minimum.

Cruising was an experience most of Mel's co-workers hoped to have an opportunity to enjoy several years down the road, when their bank accounts became more flush and their children grown. The two requirements, understandably, interdependent. Needless to say, child-rearing today hardly allows one the opportunity to possess a padded savings account.

For now, they would have to settle for a detailed account of Mel's adventure, complete with many photographs.

2

As expected, the weeks leading up to departure dragged by, at a snail's pace. Melissa, seemingly no less busy than usual, was surprised at the slow passage of time. Realizing this was a common complaint, when one was anxiously anticipating a pleasurable event, the young woman responded to the delay with her usual good humor.

Eventually, the time for leaving had arrived, plans completed without difficulty.

The evening prior to departure, Mel traveled to her aunt's estate, from where the ladies were to set out the following morning. Judith's van, a vehicle modified to accommodate her wheelchair in the upright position, was to be their mode of transportation to the airport, eliminating any need for assistance. They would park the vehicle in the available lot for the extent of their journey, thus making it accessible to them upon their return.

Melissa's drive to her aunt's residence was spent in contemplation, regressing back to similar treks she had made over these country roads. Her thoughts revolved around the woman with whom she planned to experience the delights of cruising.

Judith Carson was a lady of sixty-eight years, who looked younger than her stated age. She had, until recently, maintained a very active lifestyle. Since her heart attack, five years previously, followed by persistent anginal episodes, her activity level had diminished appreciably.

Her wheelchair was a necessary commodity, due to the increased debilitating effects of multiple sclerosis. Though afflicted with this ailment as a young adult Judith had, other than occasional exacerbations, been spared any serious impairment from the disorder, until recently. With the deterioration in her general health, the MS had intensified, resulting in a degree of immobility. Thus, the wheelchair.

Mel's aunt was a handsome woman who, throughout her life, had established stringent health habits. By conscientiously following a proper diet, she had maintained weight control. It had long been her policy to refrain from smoking; and she consumed alcohol sparingly.

Thus the onset of heart disease had been as much a blow to her ego as to her physical well-being, feeling that anyone who had been as health-conscious as she, did not deserve such misfortune.

Dr. Adams however, explained to her that an individual with a strong family history of heart disease had little chance of totally escaping its influence. The only saving grace preventing Judith from being effected, at an earlier age, had been the care she had exercised.

Melissa's mother (Judith's sister) had been less fortunate, expiring at the age of fifty-five, from a massive coronary.

Rebecca Sommers had smoked from early childhood. A habit she had diligently attempted to conquer, without success. Her diet had contained a high level of cholesterol (a consequence of living on a farm), and she had always carried an extra twenty pounds. This combination of risk factors made a myocardial infarction inevitable.

Never having been the type of individual to permit her physical restrictions to keep her from enjoying life to the fullest, Judith simply made what adjustments her various ailments dictated and persevered. Such was the case with her latest affliction.

Melissa had enjoyed a close bond with her aunt, since childhood. A bond which had strengthened, with the loss of Rebecca. Since that time, Judith had stepped into the maternal role, filling the void superbly.

Judith recognized many similarities between herself and her sister's child, both in looks and personality. The irony of this was the total lack of common ground Judith shared with her own children. Their relationship was best described as strained. This inability to communicate effectively with her offspring, disturbed the woman a good deal.

Motherhood was one facet of her life where Judith was dissatisfied with her personal performance. To her credit, she had made attempts to rectify the unpleasantness between herself and her children. Unfortunately, Donald and Suzanne did not appear receptive to overtures, on their mother's part, to promote a more amicable understanding.

Any indication of familial love had long been discarded; choosing instead the pursuit of loftier ambitions. The primary goal being immense wealth and position. This goal had been attained, but at what cost? Was it worth the price they had forced themselves to pay? Perhaps, for now. However, Melissa felt certain that, with time, they were sure to acknowledge that monetary riches, no matter how great, were seldom enough to sustain one when the path became rocky.

Judith would be the first to admit most of the problems she was presently experiencing with her children, were a direct result of their upbringing. Having lived a monetarily deprived childhood, Judith, fortunate enough to marry a very wealthy man, was able to cater to her children's every whim which, regrettably, she had done. By doing so she exhibited to them, from a very early age, the advantages of being disgustingly rich.

On the other hand, Kenneth Sommers (Melissa's father) had been a farmer and times were seldom easy. With nine mouths to feed and bodies to clothe, money was always scarce. Nonetheless, Melissa's developmental years were carefree, as her parents kept their financial worries to themselves.

Food, though never fancy, was nutritious, as they lived, for the most part, off the land. The sale of produce and butchered livestock provided the means by which all other essentials were purchased.

Hand-me-downs were an integral part of Mel's growing up; a source of constant teasing and ridicule at the local school. Mel minded the teasing, but her intense pride would not permit her to let it show.

Responsibility was taught early, as there were many chores involved with the management of a profitable farming enterprise and everyone had their assigned duties. It was the time spent together, after the accomplishment of their chores, which made up for the fatigue brought on by hard work. Father would get out the guitar and the family participated in a singsong. Some evenings they engaged in a rousing card game, or one of Mel's brothers would make the rounds, challenging all takers to a checkers tournament.

Recreation on the farm involved a good deal of physical exertion. Hockey and skating were indulged in, only after clearing the local pond of its usual two to three inches of snow. The same pond was converted to a swimming hole during the summer months, the winter's twenty minute distance noticeably shortened by the absence of skates and hockey sticks to carry.

It bothered Mel that most children today would never be

given the opportunity to enjoy the experiences that were part of her daily life as a young girl.

Aromas, such as fresh pie or bread baking, and stew simmering on a wood stove. The smell of the country air and how it reflected the changing seasons.

To be able to appreciate the feeling of entering the house, after walking home from school in a snowstorm, with the wood stove providing a warmth and comfort penetrating every fiber of one's being, seemingly reaching your very soul.

The sense of accomplishment one felt when the crops produced a plentiful yield and you knew you had an active role in attaining that much sought for result.

The joy you experienced when Mother's quilt won the blue ribbon at the county fair. Though you are able to recognize the squares you sewed, she refuses to acknowledge any imperfection in your stitch.

Playing in the snow so long your mittens are wet; hands encased in them numb from the cold. Entering the house barely long enough to change to another mismatched pair, before venturing out again. Of course, children always knew, once they decided they had enough fresh air for one day, the cup of hot chocolate awaiting them could remove any chill.

Getting up on a winter's morning and dressing for school under the bed covers. Or racing to be the first to reach the kitchen stove to clad yourself, while protected by its warm cloak. Being first was imperative as it was virtually impossible for any more than three children to get dressed, at one time, within the immediate vicinity of the range.

Coasting with her siblings, under the moonlight, produced some of Mel's fondest memories. The only disappointing factor: the length of time it took to walk up the icy road, dragging her sled, in contrast to the frightening speed reached descending that same slippery road, on that same sled.

All these events and emotions were permanently embedded in Mel's memory. Experiences she would not have missed for the world. Hand-me-downs were a small price to pay for what she had received in return. The wealth the Sommers had given to their children was an abundance of love. And, when all is said and done, isn't that, essentially, what life is all about?

Although Donald and Suzanne's younger years were spent, at the opposite end of the financial spectrum, their parents had attempted to instill in them the proper value of money. These teachings, however, had drastically missed the mark. Donald and Suzanne were of the opinion that extreme wealth was their undeniable right, not merely a case of good fortune and dedication on the part of their ancestors.

Howard's father had been a self-made man, starting his own advertising business at a young age. His hard work and diligence had paid off and the business flourished.

Being an only child, Howard had inherited the multi-million dollar company. Though lacking his father's financial savvy, Howard possessed the same work ethic and had a good sense of what appealed to the general populace in the way of advertising. Howard's abilities, in combination with Judith's fine-toned business skills, made the successful advancement of the agency inevitable.

The natural assumption would be for the company, upon Judith's death, to be passed on to one of her children. This was an event they anxiously awaited.

Judith owned the bulk of the shares and, despite her ill health, maintained supervisory control. The assistant manager, a young man by the name of Timothy Hudson, oversaw the ongoing activities, reporting directly to Judith. This arrangement proved satisfactory and would remain unchanged; the owner's will clearly stipulating continuation of the present setup. One alteration would be evoked by Judith's death: transfer of the company's ownership to her niece, Melissa Sommers. A fact known only to Judith and her lawyer, Raymond Currie.

Judith's children would be handsomely compensated, in the event of her passing. She had no intention, however, of allowing the business she and her husband had worked at so assiduously, to fall by the wayside as a result of poor management. Such, she believed, would be the case, if control of Carson Agency was left in the incompetent hands of either of her children.

Judith had no qualms about Mel's inexperience in the field of advertising. With her natural flair for business and Timothy's guidance, Judith was convinced Melissa would be able to cope admirably. A conscientious individual, Mel could be relied upon to familiarize herself with all pertinent data relevant to her assumption of the appointed task of managing an advertising firm.

3

The tree-lined lane, leading to the Carson estate, was always a welcoming sight to Melissa. Despite the vastness of the property, she did not feel overwhelmed by its grandeur. Many happy summer vacations had been spent, amid the splendor and majesty of the mansion. Melissa had passed the hours horseback riding; swimming in the Olympic size pool; and taking long walks on the grounds with her aunt.

Upon initially purchasing the mansion, Judith had resisted her husband's inclination to employ the services of an interior decorator, deciding instead to oversee all renovations personally.

Over a period of time, she had carefully selected pieces of art from fine galleries and private collections. She had, successfully, intermingled paintings by the great artists with more modern pieces by local artisans. Her fondness for antique furniture was clearly demonstrated by the vast array of such items located throughout the residence.

Judith expressed a great deal of satisfaction over the end result. A sense of accomplishment she would have missed, had she taken a less active role in the process. She knew the final effect achieved would have lacked the atmosphere she had wished to create. Even Howard was forced to admit the effect was stunning.

As Mel rang the doorbell, she noted the flower beds were beginning to bloom. Within another month they would be alive with color. Gardening was the activity Judith missed most, since her confinement to the wheelchair.

A young girl Mel's age, Carmelita, answered the doorbell. Anna, Carmelita's mother, had worked for the Carsons since their marriage. With her advancing years, Anna had taken on the duties of chief cook; her daughter assuming the more rigorous role of maid. All parties were satisfied with the new delegation of responsibilities, the changes resulting in minimal disruption to the household.

Carmelita held a degree in business administration. Despite this, she preferred to remain in Judith's employ. A chief factor in her decision was the generous salary she earned at her present post. It was unlikely that she could do better, even with her qualifications, holding down an office position.

Mrs. Carson had offered the girl the opportunity to work at the agency for a similar salary. Had it not been for the extra attraction of working side-by-side with Anna, Carmelita would have accepted the position. However, being very close to her mother, she preferred to remain at the estate.

The salary which Judith paid her house staff was a constant source of friction between her and her children. Donald and Suzanne felt that the amount was excessive for, as they expressed it, "mere servants."

Carmelita greeted her friend with a hug, "Mother has prepared your favorite, chicken dinner with all the fixings, including apple pie for dessert. You haven't eaten, have you?"

"Anna would never forgive me, if I arrived in any state other than famished. Believe me, I have ample room for one of her delectable dinners." Melissa announced her desire to do justice to the cook's culinary expertise. The aromas wafting in from the kitchen reminded her just how hungry she was, having not eaten since early morning.

Following greetings all around, the feast was served. As usual, the meal sated everyone's hunger. Anna was noted for making the most simple fare a work of art. Tonight's offering being no exception.

Considering Judith's preference for roast chicken, Melissa was puzzled, and somewhat alarmed, by her aunt's obvious lack of appetite. While drinking coffee with Judith in the study, after the others had made their excuses and gone their separate ways, Melissa remarked on her observations.

"Judith, are you not feeling well? You hardly touched your dinner."

"Food has lost its appeal for me as of late," admitted her aunt. "In fact, I have not been feeling well for several months. The chief reason for this trip is to revitalize my engines."

"Why didn't you tell me? Is Dr. Adams aware you have been feeling poorly?"

"He is aware, but can find no explanation for my symptoms. I, on the other hand, know the reason for my declining health. To put it simply, my dear, I believe someone is trying to poison me."

"What in the world gives you that idea?" exclaimed Mel, shocked by Judith's declaration.

"I am not stupid, Melissa. Donald and Suzanne have recently returned from a business trip. During their absence, I began to improve. My appetite increased and my strength was coming back. The abdominal discomfort I had been experiencing had dissipated and I appeared to be on the road to recovery. My health has rapidly deteriorated, since their return. Logically, that implies that they are, in some way, responsible for my difficulties. One effective way to create the problems I have been noticing is through the administration of poison."

"That sounds to me to be a bit obvious on their part. Surely, if what you are saying is true, they would be more careful to avoid implicating themselves. If the only time you feel unwell is when they are present, that definitely narrows down the list of likely candidates, should a case of poisoning be suspected."

"My children, though devious, are not particularly bright. They probably assumed I would blame my MS for any new symptoms I was experiencing."

"The symptoms you describe are not those associated with MS. It is possible, though, that you are suffering side effects from some of your medications. Digoxin, for example, commonly causes gastrointestinal disturbances, if it reaches toxic levels. Have you undergone any recent blood tests to determine if you have a therapeutic level of those drugs in your system?"

"Dr. Adams sent me for tests of that nature. The results were normal. He also checked for poisonous substances, but everything came back negative. That is not of much solace to me.

"Research which I have conducted indicates that blood tests done to detect poisonous substances are not always totally definitive. A negative reading may simply mean that there was not enough poison in my bloodstream at the time of testing; thus escaping detection. It is also true that some agents cannot be traced by routine testing; especially if administered in small amounts, over an extended period of time. As I said, my children are devious. They would research the subject, being careful to select a poison which, while being effective, is difficult to trace."

"I hope you are mistaken, Judith," remarked Mel.

"So do I, my dear."

At this juncture Melissa signified to her aunt that the eavesdropper, who had been present during the course of their conversation, appeared to have vacated the area. Though uncertain as to the interloper's identity, the ladies were pleased that someone had responded to the bait they had set (by leaving the study door ajar). Shortly after entering the room the women had heard low breathing noises outside the door, confirming their belief that another individual was secretly interested in what was being discussed.

After an extensive perusal of the immediate vicinity, to ensure absence of further uninvited listeners, Mel reassured her aunt that they were, indeed, alone. With this guarantee, Judith initiated the primary topic she wished to discuss with her niece. Subject matter which proved to be both intriguing and unexpected. As Judith outlined the aspects of her plan, the need for secrecy became evident, as did Melissa's role in the scheme. A part the younger woman, while not eager to play, was forced to admit was essential for the plan to have any chance of success.

4

After a fitful sleep (disturbed by Judith's revelations), Melissa awoke early. The guest room she presently occupied had always been her favorite. It was a spacious, cheerful room with a large four-poster bed as the focal point. The log cabin quilt adorning the bed added character, as did the tastefully displayed pictures decorating the walls. In one corner sat an antique rocking chair, creating its own comforting ambiance.

Since the bedroom provided the luxury of an en suite, Melissa could indulge in her usual early morning shower, without fear of disturbing other members of the household. Next she chose her attire for the day. The selection of kelly green cotton pants with a light print blouse appeared appropriate dress, with a warm cardigan to combat the initial coolness.

Exiting the room, she descended the staircase and was drawn to the kitchen by the tantalizing aroma of freshly brewed coffee. I'm not the only early bird, she reasoned.

Donald, Judith's son was the other early riser. "Would you care for a cup?" he offered, pointing to the coffeepot.

"Yes, thank you. That would be delightful," responded Mel, grateful for the offer of the stimulating beverage. Mel was an individual who appreciated, to the point of requiring, a coffee upon arising. Despite this fact, she was not one unable to be civil, prior to ingesting it. Several of her friends fit, very aptly, into the latter category.

"I'm pleased you are accompanying Mother on the cruise," announced Donald. "It is reassuring to know she is traveling with someone she trusts and who is trained to take proper care of her. Medically speaking, that is. I get the impression she has not been feeling well recently."

"Yes, she admitted as much to me, after some prompting. Her chief complaints seem to be loss of appetite, abdominal discomfort and general malaise." Mel carefully scrutinized her cousin's features for any sign suggesting a guarded reaction. She had to admit the only expression noted was that of genuine concern. Mel was adept in the art of interpreting non-verbal communication. She was also a firm believer in the ability to visualize a person's guilt or innocence, by looking directly into their eyes. In this instance, she found neither method revealed any indication that Donald was attempting to hide something. If the man was instrumental in contributing to his mother's failing health, he certainly was proficient at displaying an innocent facade.

"Yes, the dear lady has definitely been under the weather. I suggested she postpone the trip until such time as she was feeling better. I'm sure you know what sort of response that evoked. She flatly refused. As much as told me to mind my own business. You know how obstinate she can be when she gets her mind set on something." Mel had to agree that Donald's assessment of his mother's personality was an accurate one.

"How is the company doing?" Mel asked, changing the subject.

"Very well, thank you," replied Donald. "The business appears to be on firm footing. Suzanne and I have recently returned from a trip abroad. The aim of our expedition was to develop new contacts and present some new ideas to our European clientele. Several of the companies with whom we hold an advertising account have their head offices in foreign countries. Thus, it is good business practice to approach the family office, on occasion, just to touch base. It also serves to develop a better rapport with those individuals with whom you do business."

"I imagine your work for the agency keeps you very busy."

"Indeed, that it does. One of the drawbacks of working for a family business is that one feels an increased sense of obligation for the overall success of the company, rarely permitting a nine-to-five work schedule. It is that sense of duty that also interferes with a normal family life."

"Speaking of your family, I have not seen them since my arrival. Are they away?"

"They are visiting Connie's folks for a few days, prior to the boys returning to school."

Shortly, in Mel's wake, Anna reported for duty to prepare the family's breakfast. Initially the cook appeared upset by the presence of others in her kitchen, though quickly hid her disapproval. Declining Mel's offer for assistance with the food preparation, Anna began. In short order the titillating redolence of frying bacon, combined with the pleasing smell of a freshly perking pot of coffee, permeated the air. Mel, unaccustomed to partaking of a large breakfast, was astonished by the degree of hunger she felt.

Anna was the first to comment on Judith's absence, noting that the lady had not summoned for assistance. Normally an early riser, Judith had developed a built-in alarm clock, to awaken her when her medication was due. Her first dose of anti-arrhythmic was taken at six A.M., the hour now being seven. Anna reminded the others that Mrs. Carson preferred to start her day within a half-hour after awakening.

"I'll check on her," offered Melissa. "Since she has not been feeling well, she may have decided to sleep late, knowing she had a strenuous day in store. What with the trip and all."

Donald accompanied his cousin, stating that it was easier to help Judith into her wheel chair, if two able-bodied individuals were present.

Receiving no response from two firm knocks, Melissa entered her aunt's room with Donald following her lead. The woman lying in the bed remained unresponsive as the two advanced toward her. Mel promptly checked Judith's pulse, informing Donald that it was weak and thready. The man needed no encouragement to summon an ambulance.

The emergency vehicle arrived in under ten minutes to transport Judith to Oakville Memorial. Melissa chose to travel in the back of the ambulance with her aunt, the other family members occupying the car driving a short distance behind.

Despite extensive medical attention, Dr. Adams advised the family of the unsuccessful resuscitative measures, one hour post arrival.

"I don't understand," declared Donald. "I know Mother has not been feeling up to par, but I had no idea it was a life threatening situation. What, exactly, was the cause of death?"

"That has not, as yet, been established. As usual, in the case of an unexplained death, an autopsy will be performed. Once I have the results, you will be notified." With this, Dr. Adams excused himself and departed, leaving the mourners alone with their grief.

As expected, Suzanne's reaction to the news of her mother's death was an emotional display worthy of an Academy Award. Her performance was filled with sentiment, but, not surprisingly, lacked any sincere sorrow. Anyone unfamiliar with the background surrounding the Carson clan, nevertheless, would have unquestionably been won over by the grieving daughter production. It was a shame, Mel concluded, that Suzanne had failed to pursue an acting career. What a waste, considering the woman's flair for the dramatic.

In direct contrast to his sister, Donald showed little evidence of emotion. Knowing the man, as she did, Mel was aware that he preferred to keep his feelings to himself. A tendency alien to his sister. Mel deduced that this trait was sure to create innumerable advantages in his business dealings.

Suzanne continued to moan and weep incessantly. Approaching his sister, Donald was obviously becoming somewhat irritated with her behavior. "For God's sake, Suzanne, get a grip on yourself. None of us are falling for your alligator tears. More importantly, no one else is watching."

"You are very cruel, Donald. Just because you and Mother were never close, you have no right to assume that my relationship with her was equally as cold." Suzanne sniveled, while surveying the immediate vicinity to see if her audience had indeed abandoned her.

"We both know that the only thing you are close to is money." Donald continued to berate his sister. "With Mother's death, the prospect of being even closer to the object of your desire is, no doubt, making you weak with anticipation."

Suzanne could not, within herself, deny the validity of her brother's words. Outward expression was a different matter. His comments only succeeded in eliciting an increase in the rate and volume of her sobs.

"When will we receive news of the results of the autopsy?" Donald turned his attention to Melissa, ignoring his sister's augmented outburst.

"An autopsy is normally done within twenty-four hours. We should hear something by tomorrow afternoon, at the latest," Mel answered.

"I suggest we go home and prepare funeral arrangements," recommended Donald. Ever the businessman, he wished to get on with the most pressing matters.

"My understanding is that Judith has already taken care of the details for her funeral." Melissa found the fact that Donald was unaware of his mother's prearranged plans a trifle unexpected.

Following a brief period of hesitation Donald responded.

"That being the case, Raymond, the family lawyer, will have documentation of the details." It was obvious, at least to Mel, that her cousin was embarrassed over his ignorance of his mother's prearranged funeral. "He is a very competent attorney. Mother often spoke of how impressed she was with his abilities, finding him to have a sound head on his shoulders. Comments she never used to describe her own son and my potential to manage the agency.

"Mother assumed that my only interests lay with money. That is undeniably true of my sister. For my part, other things do excite me. From time to time."

The group left the hospital; Suzanne appearing a good deal calmer. Mel found herself wondering how much of the woman's improved mental status was due to the lack of sympathy her emotional display had evoked.

The first order of business was notification of family and friends of Judith's passing. Raymond was contacted and the prearranged funeral plans were confirmed. The lawyer suggested scheduling the reading of the will for the evening following the service.

"That will be fine," agreed Donald, "as it is simply a formality. We are aware of the contents."

"I wouldn't be so sure if I were you," advised the attorney. "Judith made some last minute alterations in her will. This new document replaces all preexisting testaments."

"I do not understand what you are implying, Ray. Could you possibly be more specific about these changes?"

"Everything will become clear when the will is read. I just thought I should warn you not to count your acquisitions until they are firmly in your grasp." Following this closing statement, Ray said his good-byes.

Donald reasoned there was little justification for alarm. After all, it was unlikely the alterations would be of any major consequence. Surely their mother would have informed them of any significant changes she had been considering. However, to avoid any further outcry from Suzanne, her brother chose to refrain from repeating Raymond's warning.

"Do you think, since they are doing an autopsy, they actually suspect foul play in Mother's death?" asked Suzanne, her question greeting Donald when he rejoined the others.

"An autopsy is required by law, in the event of an unexplained death, especially when the circumstances are suspicious." Mel was a bit perturbed over the need to reiterate information Dr. Adams had already provided.

"What do you mean, suspicious circumstances? Mother has been unwell for years, especially since her heart attack. Lately, she has been more incapacitated, due to her MS. Surely her death was caused by one of those factors."

"Obviously, the doctors feel that her existing heath conditions were not responsible for her death. Her cardiac status was stabilized with medication and MS, though debilitating, is rarely fatal. The only way to determine the actual cause of death is through a post-mortem."

"You mean to tell me that it does not bother any of you," Suzanne spread her arms in a gesture to encompass everyone in the room, "that they will be cutting Mother up?"

"Not if that is the only way to discover what killed her," announced Donald.

Suzanne, again aware of the lack of support directed toward her, decided it was best to drop the subject. While not being noted for her intelligence, she did not lack the basic instincts of self-preservation inherent in most individuals. Instincts which normally lead people to back away from an argument they have no hope of winning, especially when they are outnumbered. For once, Suzanne's reaction was appropriate.

5

Early the next day, as promised, Dr. Adams phoned with the autopsy results. "The drug scan showed a particularly high concentration of arsenic. A very effective poison. If administered in small amounts it causes nausea, abdominal pain and general malaise. A large dose will almost certainly cause death. The onset of which would be fairly rapid. From the high concentration of the drug found in her system, she must have received a lethal dose within a few hours of her death."

Donald, who had taken the doctor's call, was momentarily at a loss for words, as the full implication of the disclosure hit home. When he regained his composure, his response denoted the disbelief he felt. "You mean, Dr. Adams, that Mother was murdered!"

"That appears to be the case. It is unlikely that she would consume the poison voluntarily."

"If someone gave it to her, wouldn't she notice an unpleasant taste?"

"Most people are under the assumption that poison is always bitter. That, of course, is true of some substances. Arsenic, however, is both tasteless and odorless. Which is why it is such an excellent agent. Anyone receiving it is totally unaware of its presence.

"The police have been notified of these findings and they will, no doubt, be in touch with you."

The peal of the doorbell signified the prompt arrival of the authorities. Donald, having finished his conversation with the doctor, admitted the officers.

"I assume you know why we are here?" the policeman spoke with a tone which the company translated as accusatory.

"Yes. Dr. Adams called. There must be some mistake. No one here is capable of murder." Donald's voice was firm.

Mel took note, yet again, of her cousin's changing deportment. There was an air of self-confidence and strength, characteristics previously lacking.

Suzanne's attitude toward the police was aggressive. "This is insane! How can you honestly believe that we could kill our own mother?"

"It has been known to happen, Miss. Actually, we are not accusing you of anything. At least, not yet. In the event of a murder, a fact as you know has been confirmed by the autopsy, we have no recourse but to explore all details leading up to the individual's death. We have found, through experience, that the best place to begin is with those who were closest to the victim. In this case, that leads us to all of you. If you will answer a few questions, we will make this as painless as possible and be out of your way."

"Well I, for one, resent your questions, not to mention your insinuations. That says nothing of the ill manners you have displayed by disturbing our privacy in this, our time of grief." Suzanne was intent on verbalizing her displeasure. However, if her main objective was to make the policemen uncomfortable by her oration, she failed miserably in the attempt.

"We apologize for the imposition, Miss." The man kept his manner polite, despite the woman's rude rejoinder. "We have no objections to conducting this interview at the station, if you prefer."

"I will do no such thing!" Suzanne was aghast at the mere suggestion of being escorted to a police station for questioning. What would her friends say, should they find out about the visit? It was not a question of whether or not they would learn of the embarrassing event. The only question was how long it would take for the news to get around. Knowing her acquaintances and the contacts they had, it would not take long.

"Very well. In that case, am I to assume that we are free to continue here?" the policeman asked. With an affirmative nod from the agitated woman (about all she could manage at this juncture, having not fully recovered from the invitation of a trip to a police station), he proceeded.

"It seems fairly obvious that no one, of their own volition, would knowingly introduce arsenic into their system. Therefore, it follows, that someone had been administering the substance to Mrs. Carson.

"We have learned that your mother had been feeling under the weather for several months. Our belief is that she had been receiving small amounts of the poison for a similar duration of time. If, as we suspect, she initially attributed her declining health to her existing ailments, it is difficult to estimate when the poisoning first began.

"Mrs. Carson's planned cruise required our perpetrator to speed up their attack. The reason for this would be twofold. One, if the lady were absent for a month she would no longer be accessible to them. Secondly, once away her health was sure to improve. A chance those wishing her removal could not afford to take. They knew her resultant improvement would eliminate any doubt from her mind as to what was causing her physical symptoms. She was certain to realize that some external force was at work.

"I imagine they were becoming frustrated over the length of time it was taking for the slow administration of the poison to be effective. They had little choice, however. Had they administered the arsenic in larger doses, they risked detection.

"Her scheduled trip put a cog in the works. If she were away for the scheduled month, it would require starting over from the beginning, gradually building up the level of arsenic in her bloodstream. No, the only way to insure success was to finish the job, before she had a chance to escape their clutches. Thus, the lethal dose was given on the night prior to her departure. They knew they were taking a risk by administering the lethal dose, but they apparently believed it was a risk worth taking. They could not afford to wait any longer.

"If anyone can detect a hole in our theory, please feel free to comment." The detective deliberately directed this statement toward Suzanne (as if that lady needed any encouragement to express herself).

"You can immediately cross Donald and I off your list of suspects. We have only recently returned from a trip abroad and, therefore, could not have been involved." Suzanne smugly remarked.

"Yes, we have been advised that you were indeed absent for a two week interval. Perhaps you are not aware that, during your time away, your mother began recovering from the effects of her poisoning. An improvement that rapidly disintegrated upon your return." It was apparent from Suzanne's countenance, that she was unprepared for this declaration.

"My God!" she exclaimed, "you actually do believe that we killed her."

"As I said, we are making no accusations. Just assembling the facts as they present themselves, omitting nothing. There will be a complete investigation, covering all possibilities. Of course, we have no authority to hold you here, but we prefer no one leave town until our inquiry is completed.

"Several forensic specialists will be arriving shortly to search for clues. I gather that Mrs. Carson's bedroom has been undisturbed since the body was discovered."

"Of course," confirmed Donald. "You will find everything exactly as it was."

"Very well. Now if each of you will go with one of my men, we can finish today's session and be on our way. A fact of which, I am sure, we will all be grateful." Again, the policeman turned his gaze toward Suzanne during his statement. "After questioning the family, we will interrogate the hired help.

"Ms. Sommers," he addressed Melissa, "I will speak with you here, if that is convenient?"

"Certainly, that will be fine," agreed Mel.

Donald and Suzanne were escorted from the room by the other officers. Melissa wondered which of the men would be assigned the unenviable task of speaking with Suzanne. Neither, she was certain, was eager to be delegated for that confrontation. Perhaps they would draw straws.

"By the way," the detective remaining in the room with Melissa began, "my name is Mike." By volunteering to initiate a less impersonal approach, Mel assumed the detective wished to alleviate some of the existing tension associated with the police visit. "I'm sure you understand the need for thoroughly researching the events surrounding your aunt's death."

"Yes, and I will be happy to help in any way I can. The important thing is to find out who is responsible."

"Do you have any thoughts on that yourself?" prompted Mike.

"No, sir. But, the evening prior to her death, Judith told me she suspected she was being poisoned."

"Really. If your aunt felt she was in danger, why did she not contact us? Had she done so, perhaps we could have removed the threat. "

"Denial, I think. Although she was forced to admit the possibility of someone wishing her dead, she couldn't accept the actuality. As you mentioned earlier, she knew if she started to feel better once away from the estate, she would then have to acknowledge that she was indeed being poisoned. She was

prepared to go to the proper authorities, once she had something concrete to support her accusations."

"Did she say who she suspected?"

Mel was dubious whether or not to continue, not wishing
to implicate her cousins without sufficient evidence of their
involvement. Her moment of hesitation was not lost on the
policeman.

"Ms. Sommers, if you have any information which I
should be privy to, you would be well-advised to spill it."

So much for the friendly overtures, thought Melissa.

"Judith believed her children wished her dead. She was
also convinced that they were not content to wait for natural
causes to dictate the time of her passing. You see, they would
inherit everything. The prospect of independent wealth, as
Judith explained her theory, can force ordinary, nonviolent
individuals, to act in ways totally foreign to their nature.

"I must point out that she had not the slightest piece of
evidence, other than her improved health during their absence,
to support her allegations."

"Your aunt had a point, Miss. In my experience I have
found that money makes a dandy motive for murder. Do you
share your aunt's opinion about what your cousins are capable
of doing, if the occasion of obtaining their inheritance seemed
a bit too far off in the future?"

"It is difficult to imagine Suzanne doing anything that
would dirty her hands, either literally or figuratively speaking.
I'm not sure about Donald. Both of them have been accustomed to financial wealth and appear to value it highly. To
what degree, I cannot say.

"Their relationship with Judith always was a bit strained.
That is not to say that they would have wished her dead, or
would have done anything to increase the likelihood of that
occurring. To be perfectly honest, I do not know what my
cousins are capable of, when money is involved."

"They do seem a bit smug, for my tastes, especially the
woman," commented Mike.

"Yes. I think smugness is a permanent fixture with Suzanne.

Although I loved my aunt dearly, I must admit that her children's condescending attitudes stem directly from the way they were raised. Their parents, particularly Judith, spoiled them frightfully, from the time they were very small. Being poor herself as a child, Judith was determined that her offspring never want for anything. Unfortunately, she failed to realize, until it was too late, the detrimental effect wrought by her overindulgence.

"Suzanne and Donald have little tolerance for those who are not of their income bracket. Donald, however, gives recent indication of mellowing somewhat. I have noticed some rather appealing characteristics developing in him since my last visit."

"There may be a specific reason for altering his personality," suggested Mike. "Have you considered the possibility that he may be doing so to avoid suspicion in his mother's murder? Development of the 'turning over a new leaf' scenario. You have to guard against those fellows."

"I never thought of it that way." Mel admitted that the detective's interpretation of Donald's new persona, while unpleasant, was indeed plausible. "I still prefer to believe that murder is not a line either of them would cross, no matter how strong the incentive."

"It is natural to be adverse to believing that a relative could perform such a vile act, even if that person is not someone we have any great affection for," said Mike.

"The fact remains, Miss Sommers, that someone in this house killed your aunt. As the strongest motive lies with her children, it would be ludicrous for me to focus my attention elsewhere, until I have exhausted that possibility. You have conceded some uncertainty, on your part, as to what they are capable of. If, by knowing them, you cannot eliminate the possibility of their involvement, I certainly cannot exclude the likelihood that they are responsible."

As their discussion was drawing to a close, the others returned.

"If you can provide us with the whereabouts of the estate

personnel, we will question them now," requested Mike.

"Anna, the cook is presently in the kitchen. The maid, Carmelita, is engaged upstairs. Maurice, our chauffeur, can be located in the garage, where he is polishing the limos. Maria, Anna's assistant, is absent but due to return momentarily. Katherine, the manager of the estate's affairs and Mother's private secretary, is catching up on some paperwork in Mother's office." Donald provided necessary directions for the officers to locate all those individuals with whom they wished to converse. "Mr. Conrad can usually be found in the stable area. That is the complete list of our staff."

"Fine, thank you sir. We will proceed. We appreciate everyone's cooperation in this matter."

"Not at all, Officer. Only too glad to help," declared Donald. Suzanne's eyes shot daggers at her brother. But, as usual, they missed their mark.

6

Katherine Watson liked her job. More importantly, she needed her job. Now, with Judith's death, her job would be gone.

As her duties involved, for the most part, working closely with Mrs. Carson, her employer's death effectively eliminated any need for a private secretary, or someone to manage the estate's affairs. That was the rationale that would be used, when they gave her the boot.

Even if the younger Carsons felt there was a need for such a staff member, they would hire someone new. Someone more easily controlled.

Katherine had never gotten along with Suzanne. She knew of few who did. Suzanne would make it her personal responsibility to insure her adversary was no longer employed.

But then, maybe not. Not if Katherine played her cards right. Not if she used the interesting information she had recently learned about Ms. Carson, to sway the woman to her way of thinking. Some people might call it blackmail. Blackmail, such an ugly word. Katherine saw it differently. She viewed it as a means to an end. She relied on the considerable income she now received and knew it would be impossible to find another position paying on a par with her present post. It wasn't just for her. She had Cody to think of. His father made no effort to assist her. Why should he? He had never wanted the child in the first place. Suzanne would have to see things her way.

Katherine's thoughts were interrupted by a knock on the office door. With her reply, "Come in. It's open," Detective Rawlins entered. "May I speak with you for a moment?" the policeman politely inquired.

"Certainly, sir."

"I am here to look into the death of your former employer. As you may know, we have established that Mrs. Carson died as a result of arsenic poisoning. Since it is indisputable that this act had to have been accomplished by someone close to her, we are centering our investigation here. Do you know of any information which could lead us to the identity of the guilty party?"

"I'm sorry, Detective. I don't think I can be of much assistance. I only work here through the day, nine to five. As I do not reside on the estate, I am unfamiliar with the daily routines of the members of the household. Questioning the cook and her daughter, Anna and Carmelita Gonzales would, no doubt, be more worthwhile. They live in the servants quarters and are more closely associated with the other staff and family members."

"How long have you worked for Mrs. Carson?"

"Seven years now."

"Did you like the woman?"

"Very much."

"What, exactly, does your job entail?"

"I manage the affairs of the estate, pay staff salaries and household expenses. It is my job to make certain the staff perform their duties satisfactorily. I handle all relevant correspondence, other than what falls into the personal classification. In short, it is my responsibility to ensure the smooth running of the estate."

"What will you do now, with Mrs. Carson gone?"

"The estate will still need to be managed. As Mr. and Ms. Carson work at the agency, they will hardly be able to handle my duties as well." Katherine neglected to mention her fear that the duties would be assigned to someone else. After all, once Suzanne saw things her way, that may change. It was prudent to go along with that assumption. It prevented confusion and removed the necessity of thinking up a logical explanation as to why she was kept on.

"I see. Do you know of anyone who would wish Mrs. Carson's removal?"

"That is not for me to say."

"You have your suspicions?"

"Yes. Though, it would be unfair, not to mention unwise, for me to voice them, with total absence of proof."

"I understand where you are coming from. Your job could be on the line if you were to implicate certain people."

"I'm glad you see my point, Detective."

"It would be impossible not to, given the obtrusive personality of Ms. Carson. Thank you for your time."

"Not at all. Sorry I could not be of more help."

"You can hardly be expected to provide more information than what you know. And, as you say, suspicions are of little use without proof to support them."

If he only knew my true motivation for remaining silent, Katherine thought. He might not be so understanding.

Suzanne's disposition was less than cheerful following the officers' departure.

"This situation is deplorable! To have the unmitigated gall to come into our home and accuse us of having killed our own mother. I think we should notify Raymond immediately and ask him to speak with that man's superior, demanding that he does not return."

"Suzanne, there is little Ray can do. You seem to have difficulty grasping the fact that this is a murder investigation. The police are well within the bounds of their authority to question whomever they please. You'll just have to grin and bear it." Donald's patience had been depleted by his sister's exaggerated displays of self-pity.

"I cannot understand why you are taking all of this so calmly, Donald. They are treating us like common criminals. Are they unaware of our social standing in this community? People of our breeding should be exempt from tactics such as bullying."

"I doubt if our social standing, as you put it, makes much of an impression on them. On the contrary, our wealth may serve as an irritant. They may wish to prove that people in our position are not above the law.

"Besides, asking a few questions is not usually considered bullying. Personally, I am somewhat amazed by your reaction. Mother has been murdered. Are you not the least bit interested in discovering by whose hand the act was committed?"

Though Donald appeared to be sincere, Melissa remembered Detective Rawlins' warning, cautioning her against reading too much into his conduct.

Recognizing his sister's desire to continue the debate, Donald stated, with intensity, "I do not wish to discuss this any further." Following this announcement, he departed, leaving Melissa with Suzanne, an uncomfortable position in which to find herself and one in which she had no intention of remaining any longer than proper manners prescribed.

"And what is your view of these developments? You probably believe we did it." With Donald having left the room, Suzanne turned her attack on the only remaining occupant, other than herself.

"It is not up to me to make a judgment. Your mother did express some concern over her failing health. She was convinced she was being poisoned. Like your brother, I too wish to learn who is responsible and make them pay for what they did.

"My advice to you is to cooperate with the police in their investigation. Or, at the very least, try to be less antagonistic toward them. Presenting an abrasive attitude may only serve to make you appear more guilty." Mel tended to be outspoken and blunt with her cousin, as she had found diplomacy ineffective in past dealings with her.

"I don't recall asking for your advice. You and Donald may do as you please. I have no intention of standing by and allowing the police to treat me in this fashion. If Donald will not contact Raymond, I will do so myself."

Melissa was forced to evaluate Suzanne's rendition of the maligned victim to be a competent one. Many people would be convinced she was being harassed and persecuted.

"I am not accustomed to be treated in such a fashion," she continued.

"None of us are!" exploded Mel, finding herself, as Donald before her, at the end of her rope where Suzanne was concerned. To avoid further exchange and resultant expressions of anger, Mel, too, departed the scene.

As she had stated was her intention, Suzanne notified Raymond of the day's events. Though promising to look into the situation he reiterated what Mel and Donald had already said, "There isn't much that can be done. They appear to be acting appropriately, under the circumstances. I would caution you against presenting an abrasive manner toward them. Any sign of antagonism on your part will only tend to make them more suspicious of you."

"That is what Melissa said. But, you know me, Raymond. I have never been the most patient person."

"I know, Susie. Just try to hang in there. I'll do what I can to make it easier." Raymond was the only individual, other than her father, who had ever called her Susie. She rather liked it.

Feeling somewhat calmer, after speaking with the attorney, Suzanne briefly considered apologizing to the others, then amended the idea, deciding that they would doubt her earnestness were she to so something so out of character. If she were prepared to humble herself enough to apologize, she wanted some assurance that she would not be wasting her time by doing so. It was best to wait until such time as they had smoothed their ruffled feathers and were more receptive to her peaceful overtures.

"I will never understand why I am so attracted to such a self-absorbed female." Raymond admonished himself for his increasing, though unrequited, love for Suzanne Carson. "I must be a masochist."

Suzanne's message was succeeded by another of female origin, though indubitably, one of greater significance. "Are things progressing as expected?" The initial query was given, prior to any form of greeting.

"Shouldn't we at least say 'Hello'?" scolded Raymond, albeit respectfully.

"Of course," laughed the woman. "Hello, Raymond. Well, are they?"

This time it was the lawyer's turn to chuckle. "Yes, so far everything has advanced without a hitch. The funeral will be held tomorrow. The remainder of the plan depends on Melissa."

"She will do fine," reassured his contact.

"I hope so. It is a lot to expect of one person. If someone discovers our scheme, we could be putting her in grave danger." Raymond had previously adamantly voiced his disapproval of the stratagem. After much persuasion on the part of his accomplices, he was finally convinced of the merits of the plot, devious though it was. He had vainly hoped they could have pursued a different course of action but, with Judith's planned cruise, time was of the essence. The plan they had chosen had been selected based on the potential for success. The verdict was reached democratically. He had been given an opportunity to suggest an alternate method but, with such short notice, had been incapable of devising anything his associates thought could be carried out successfully.

With any luck, results would be achieved quickly, and the need for secrecy past.

7

Judith's funeral was well-attended. Mel was not surprised by the large turnout. Her aunt was widely respected in the community. She had displayed a strong sense of civic duty: actively participating in local affairs when able, contributing sizable charitable donations and, generally, doing her part to develop the area to its fullest potential.

The service was reverent, though lacked the somber atmosphere one normally associates with such an occasion. The minister, a personal friend of the family, was adept at verbalizing the emotions of his congregation, a competence which explained his immense popularity among the members of his flock. This capability was not often found in one so young.

At close of the service, those in attendance, reflected, though disconcertedly, on what a pleasant funeral it had been.

"I'm sure Judith would have wanted you to feel heartened by the service. That was her intention." The minister removed any lingering doubt in the minds of the congregation over how Judith would have interpreted, what they felt to be, an abnormal reaction.

Melissa was the only person who gave indication of having observed a dark figure lurking at the back of the church, during the service. The individual was dressed in black and wore dark glasses. Upon inquiry, no one else confessed to having seen the woman. When Melissa sought her out, after the funeral, the mysterious figure had disappeared, without a trace, giving Melissa justification for questioning her own sanity.

Following the service, most of the congregation were invited to the estate for refreshments. Melissa was introduced to those of the group whom she had not formerly met. Among these was Timothy Hudson, the assistant manager of Carson Agency. Mr. Hudson was a distinguished looking young man; Mel estimating his age as early thirties. His features were best described as ruggedly handsome.

The young man's handshake was firm, a fairly accurate sign of honesty and confidence. Mel was impressed with the manner with which he conducted himself. Judith, who had prided herself on being an excellent judge of character, had evidently been equally as taken by the young man, considering the pivotal position she had assigned him in her company.

His appointment had been fiercely opposed by Judith's children, an objection supported by the board of directors. Needless to say, their vetoes were ignored. Judith pulled rank, hiring Timothy without their endorsement. The new assistant manager had filled the position perfectly, justifying his employer's faith in him and giving little ammunition for any legitimate complaints from those opposed to his appointment.

The company had not suffered under the direction of one so young and with limited managerial experience (this being the chief objection voiced). To the contrary, the agency had flourished with Timothy at the helm. Judith had found few incidents where her intervention was required. Mr. Hudson soon became noted for his proficiency in establishing, and effectively carrying out, sound business practices.

"Sorry to meet you under these circumstances, Miss Sommers. Your aunt spoke of you, in glowing terms, more times than I can remember. I was hoping we would have the chance to meet." Mr. Hudson's personality appeared to match his good looks.

"Likewise. Aunt Judith credited you with removing much of the stress from her life, through your smooth and efficient management of the company."

"Mrs. Carson was easy to work for. She was a perfectionist, but clearly stated her expectations. She asked nothing more from her employees than what she demanded from herself and she tolerated nothing less. You always knew where you stood with her. If she were satisfied with your achievements she let you know, and she informed you personally of any dissatisfaction. In my opinion that is the only way to deal fairly with those under your direction. You must make it known what level of performance you expect. A pat on the back should be given, if deserved. As should a good kick in the pants, so to speak, if it is warranted. I presume she handled her personal affairs in a similar fashion."

"For the most part. Her soft spot was her children, where she allowed a much freer rein than was wise. A mistake she, in later years, readily admitted." Mel, who inclined toward shyness when first meeting people, was astounded at how uninhibited she felt in the presence of this stranger. She conversed openly with him, as though they had been of long acquaintance.

After exchanging pleasantries upon meeting, the two parted to mingle with the crowd. During her conversations with other guests, Melissa found her attention drawn back to Timothy. On more than one occasion their eyes met. Episodes Mel found to be unsettling.

With the departure of the final visitor, the family and staff entered the den to hear the reading of the will. Due to the verification of company ownership and ease of transfer, the event could not be postponed. The significance of the will's contents was self-evident. Considering the pecuniary worth of Judith's estate, the meting out of her holdings would be substantial.

Suzanne, under the impression that this procedure was simply a formality, was in much better spirits.

"As you may, or may not know," Raymond began, instantaneously becoming the center of attention. "Judith recently instructed me to make a codicil to her will. Those specified alterations have been added, the new document reflecting the modifications she directed.

"The bulk of the estate is to be divided equally between her surviving children, specifically, Donald and Suzanne Carson. This is exclusive of one hundred thousand dollars awarded to her favorite charities, namely the Canadian Heart Foundation and the Multiple Sclerosis Society of Canada.

"There will be individual cash settlements of two hundred thousand to both Anna and Carmelita Gonzales. All remaining house and property staff will receive cash amounts proportionate to three years' wages."

There were no surprises here, Raymond thought. The next announcement was the zinger, sure to be vehemently disputed. For this reason the lawyer, wisely, introduced it as the finale. "Carson Agency is to become the sole property of Melissa Sommers, with the provision that said agency is to be under her supervisory control and is not, under any circumstances, to be sold. It is also stipulated that the name of the company remain unchanged."

Gasps of disbelief reverberated throughout the room. Raymond, anxious to finish reading the will while he held the advantage, quickly continued. The resultant silence, brought about by the unheralded news of Judith's successor, was certain to be brief. Once the initial shock wore off, he would be hard pressed to get anyone to listen to the remainder.

"Timothy Hudson will continue to manage all day-to-day business affairs of the company. At such time as Ms. Sommers can familiarize herself with the workings of the agency, she will assume the chief managerial position. Mrs. Carson judged her niece to be capable of determining at what juncture she has reached the necessary competence to function in that capacity.

"Meanwhile, Mr. Hudson will answer only to Ms. Sommers in the matter of company transactions. Donald and Suzanne Carson are to remain on staff, in their present capacities, if that is mutually acceptable.

"The agency's financial status is solvent, for now. It is, nonetheless, imperative that the transfer of ownership is accomplished smoothly and as quickly as feasibly possible, to avoid any negative ramifications resulting from a delay. Clients tend to become a bit nervous if they are unclear as to whom is in charge. A postponement in the resolution of ownership could prompt them to take their advertising business elsewhere."

"Stop right there!" Suzanne exploded, as Raymond surmised she would. "This is preposterous! If you think we will allow such a travesty to take place, you are sadly mistaken! Carson Agency has been in our family from its onset and that is where it will remain! I do not intend to permit some thieving parasite to snatch it out from under us! This will not go unchallenged!" Suzanne, once regaining her composure, had also recaptured her voice, and was now in fine form.

"Somehow," Raymond conceded, "I did not think that it would. For that reason, Judith insured the validity of the transcript and absence of any loopholes upon which you could capitalize. The document will stand up in a court of law. Of that, there is no doubt. There is nothing you can do."

"You'd be surprised what I intend to do." Suzanne's voice rose, both in pitch and volume.

"This has to be a mistake," said Donald, not yet fully recovered from the impact of the developments. "Mother clearly stated her desire to keep the company in the family. I admit, to a degree, Mel is family."

"Like hell she is!" obtruded Suzanne.

"Be quiet, Suzanne! I am speaking and I wish to be heard!" Donald glared at his sister, defying her to continue. Having never been the recipient of such a look of disdain from Donald, Suzanne thought it best to remain silent, not wishing to provoke him further. Not until she was able to evaluate his degree of hostility.

"As I said, before I was so rudely interrupted, Mel is, in part, family. She is not, however, a Carson. The agency has always had a Carson at the controls. Besides, I am already equipped with the necessary skills and expertise to competently run things. That is, of course, with Mr. Hudson's assistance. Melissa is a total greenhorn where advertising is concerned. You must have misunderstood Mother's wishes, Ray." Donald was cognizant of the fact that he was grasping at straws, a sure sign of desperation.

"Your mother's instructions were explicit. I, too, was taken aback by her decisions, but they were her decisions. She was, to my knowledge, swayed by no exterior influence. The will was carefully scrutinized by her, upon its completion, and duly signed. It is perfectly legal."

"We could contest this new will on the basis of impaired mental capacity at the time Mother made these modifications."

Donald, though equally as disturbed by the news was, for the most part, maintaining a calmer deportment than that displayed by his sister.

"I would not follow that vein if I were you, Donald," recommended the lawyer. "Your mother's mental state was unhampered by her physical impairments. A fact of which you are well aware and one which can be supported by any number of business associates who had dealings with Judith at approximately the same time as these revisions were made."

"That is debatable. We can come up with evidence to the contrary." Suzanne was tiring of remaining mute.

"You are well within your rights to try. Your chances of success, however, are remote, to say the least. The wisest course of action would be to work with your cousin, for the betterment of the agency. Any objection to the will is sure to result in months of litigation. That can only be detrimental to the agency's business dealings with clients. We must announce new management without delay. You cannot automatically place yourselves in that role, in direct opposition to your mother's bequest. Having limited shares in the agency, you have no authority to do so. Anyway, the board of directors would obstruct such a move. An opposition you could not oppose." Raymond remained patient with Suzanne, a reaction which only served to increase her hostility.

One thing the woman could not abide was having an argument with an opponent who showed no visible sign of anger. She decidedly preferred less anger than Donald had currently displayed, but some emotion was essential. If the person she confronted remained unruffled, it tended to detract from the sense of accomplishment she felt, when the disagreement was settled to her satisfaction.

"I will not settle for any less than my due," she forcefully proclaimed. "I was promised that company, and, by God, I will have it!"

"It is your prerogative to contest the will," verified Raymond. "But, as I have said, any challenge to its contents will place it in probate, which could require months to settle."

"Fine with me. I don't care if it takes years."

"Do you know what prompted these sudden changes?" asked Donald, anxious to learn what his mother's incentive may have been.

"Judith did not clarify the reason for these changes, other than to state that she felt it would be in the best interests of the agency to put Melissa in charge, in the event of her death."

"It is one thing to put Mel in charge, though I fail to see the wisdom in that decision, no offense to Mel. But why award ownership to her?" Donald's question was a valid one.

"If your mother left the company to either of you, can you honestly tell me you would not interfere with the idea of Melissa at the helm? Come now, Donald, you would be totally against it. Being the owner you could obstruct the appointment, having full vetoing power to do so," Raymond explained. "I hardly think that either of you would be content in the role of figurehead. I would say that your sister's present reaction shows the type of behavior Judith anticipated."

"You have a point." Donald reluctantly acknowledged the validity in Raymond's appraisal.

"Your trust funds are ample. With that inheritance, plus the proceeds from the sale of the estate, if you decide to go that route, properly managed, you will be financially secure for the rest of your life. I will warn you that the money will not last, however, unless strategically placed in profitable investments. There are several options you may wish to exercise toward that end." Raymond offered what he knew to be sound advice. Familiar with the younger Carsons' propensity for purchasing expensive merchandise, he assumed they could dispose of a sizable allotment of cash fairly rapidly, if they did not apply a bit of caution and self-control.

"Well, if those were indeed Mother's wishes, we will have to accept them at some juncture. It may as well be now." This remark from Judith's son elicited as spontaneous a reaction of disbelief as the disclosure of the will's contents had succeeded in doing.

"Excuse me, Donald. Surely you intend on opposing this." Suzanne was ill prepared to deal with her brother's atypical reasoning, combined with the startling facts revealed within her mother's will. She was unaccustomed to having to deal with stress (anything falling within that category normally handled by others), therefore she had not developed the coping mechanisms most people subconsciously engage, when faced with a crisis. Disappointment was also an experience she had, to date, been spared and one she could not accept gracefully.

One thing for certain, if Suzanne Carson had her heart set on a particular acquisition, she would not be appeased until that goal was attained. Be damned the consequences, or who she had to step over to claim her treasure. Now, she wanted Carson Agency. Not because she wanted to operate it, being sensible enough to realize that she had neither the skill nor the intelligence to oversee an enterprise of such magnitude. Her motivation was simple. She wanted the prestige attached to ownership of a major corporation. The task of managing the business she would assign to others, namely her brother and the current assistant manager, Timothy Hudson.

Regardless of any of the other inducements, the most important driving force behind Suzanne's opposition was her inability to permit Melissa Sommers (the woman she despised most in the world) to procure such a prize.

Suzanne's hatred toward Melissa stemmed from resentment over the close rapport her cousin had shared with Judith. A closeness which Suzanne had never been able to achieve. The fact that she had never made an effort to do so was, to her, irrelevant.

Suzanne was also incredibly jealous (though would be the last to admit that such an emotion enveloped her being) of the other woman's accomplishments. Without benefit of the financial backing that Suzanne had access to, Melissa had achieved much. At this stage in her young life, Suzanne's cousin deserved the respect she received. Another cause for bitterness on the part of Suzanne.

Allow this woman to now boast of her ownership of a major advertising agency? Never, as long as Suzanne could draw breath, would she allow that to happen.

"Suzanne, you are fully aware of Mother's competence in business matters. If, as Raymond has suggested, she guaranteed our inability to dispute the will, you can be sure that is precisely the case. We have no choice, as I see it, but to concede the inevitable." Donald's logic, though unerring, had little effect on his sister. This surprised no one.

"If that is the way you feel, Donald, so be it. I will proceed with, or without, your backing. In the meantime as the estate, at least in part, belongs to me, I want that woman out of this house." Suzanne pointed to Melissa, as if there were any doubt as to whom she made reference to.

"Suzanne, you can hardly blame Mel for Mother's decision. She was as astonished as we over the announcement. Besides, as you said, the estate is only half yours. As for my part, she is free to remain as long as she wishes." Donald, though not surprised by his sister's reaction, was embarrassed by her immaturity.

"What do you mean, I cannot blame her? Visiting Mother regularly. Ingratiating herself into the woman's affections. All the while knowing, this day would arrive. She prepared the path well."

"If that is the way you feel, though there is not an ounce of truth in it, perhaps it would be best if I were to find other accommodations until this matter is settled to everyone's satisfaction." Melissa addressed her remarks directly toward Suzanne.

"That is an excellent idea." The other woman concurred. "The sooner the better as far as I am concerned."

"That will not be necessary, Mel," countered Donald. "You mustn't let Suzanne drive you away. Unless, of course, you would feel more comfortable with other arrangements."

At this juncture, Raymond intervened, "If I may offer an opinion."

"Certainly, Ray," prompted Donald.

"I agree with Melissa that alternative accommodations would be best," continued the lawyer. "There is a lovely inn just down the road which provides exceptionally pleasant surroundings. They usually have vacancies this time of year."

"I will call immediately and make arrangements to take up temporary residence there." Melissa announced, leaving the study to make the necessary call.

With Melissa absent, Raymond made one final attempt to encourage Suzanne to come to terms with the developments. He expostulated with her the disadvantages of openly opposing her mother's wishes.

"You must realize the wisdom of providing the agency's clients with news of whom will be in charge. They are aware of Judith's death and are anxiously awaiting verification of whom they will be dealing with. It is essential we provide that information without delay."

"I have no objection to the temporary appointment of Melissa in the position, for the good of the company," stated Donald. "Knowing Mother, she thought this out carefully and must have believed it to be the wisest choice."

"And you, Susie?" asked Raymond.

"I will agree to her temporary, and I do mean temporary, appointment. As long as you know I am planning to approach a lawyer with the intention of contesting the will. You're probably right about our clients' reactions to any hint of dissension among us, or delay in naming Mother's successor."

"Yes," agreed Donald. "We must keep our internal difficulties to ourselves."

"That would be wise," said Raymond. "After all, it will be Timothy, primarily, running the agency. It will take several months for Melissa to feel comfortable taking the reins. By that time, the validity of the will is sure to be established.

"May I remind you that, as I have stated, these were, for whatever reasons, your mother's wishes."

"I have no doubt that you are following Mother's instructions," said Donald. "It would be interesting to know if anything specific prompted her decision."

"That you may never know," answered Raymond. "But, there is no point in torturing yourselves, trying to figure it out."

"Maybe you're right," agreed Donald.

"I still believe our dear cousin exerted undue pressure on Mother to encourage this action. Heaven only knows what lies she told her about us." Suzanne, despite having agreed to allow Melissa's appointment to become effective, on an impermanent basis, was not pleased with the outcome. Her concession was given only because of the detrimental effect her opposition would have on the agency. She had no intention of making Melissa's transition into her new role an easy one, that much she would make abundantly clear.

"Think what you will, Susie. I have to leave." Saying this, Raymond departed.

8

"I cannot understand how Mother could be so cruel. Leading us to assume the company would be ours, then taking it from us at the last possible moment. What a horrendous thing to do." Suzanne's reaction to the contents of the will remained unchanged. The longer she concentrated on the unexpected outcome, the more irate she became.

"It really shouldn't have come as such a shock," said Donald. "We have never been a close family. Remember how often she expressed dissatisfaction with the way we managed money. We gave her plenty of reason to lack confidence in our abilities to run a business."

"And you think Melissa will do any better? With no experience."

"No, but apparently Mother did."

"What if our opposition to the will is unsuccessful? What if she actually is awarded ownership by the courts? Do you feel you can work side by side with Timothy and Melissa? Knowing that the agency should be under our guidance."

"I am willing to try. If the courts decide the will is valid, we will have little choice. We either work side by side with them or we relinquish any part in the family business. That I will not do.

"Besides, Mel may find herself either unable or uninterested in managing the agency. A position of authority in advertising is quite different from nursing. Our cousin may feel over-whelmed by such a career move, at this stage in her life. If that were to happen, we would become the logical successors."

"Melissa does not impress me as someone given to shirking responsibility. If she thinks Mother was counting on her to take over, she will feel obligated to do so, even if the task does not particularly appeal to her." Suzanne, not known for throwing out compliments (especially when referring to her cousin), startled herself by her comment.

"True," affirmed Donald. "And, knowing Mel, if we object too strenuously, it will only cause her to dig her heels in and accept the challenge, just to prove us wrong."

"What would happen in the event of Melissa's death? Would the company belong to us?"

"Suzanne, what are you saying?" Donald's question went unanswered, as the woman of whom they spoke, at that moment, reentered the room, announcing her move to the Sunset View Inn.

"I want you to know there are no hard feelings on my part," said Donald. "I realize you had no prior knowledge of Mother's intentions. Hopefully, we can work together for the good of the agency."

"That is what I want as well," responded Melissa.

Accepting his assistance in transferring luggage to the trunk of her car, Mel shook her cousin's proffered hand, stepped into the vehicle and drove away.

Suzanne awaited her sibling's return. "I hope you are not mistaken about her reaction to all of this. There is a chance, you know, that she will thoroughly enjoy her new position. Under Timothy's tutelage, she may catch on rather quickly. You have repeatedly said how intelligent you find her to be." Suzanne's jealous nature toward Melissa was, again, coming to the fore.

"She will probably try it out for a month, as that is the extent of her leave from the hospital. She, no doubt, feels she owes that much to Mother. However, I sincerely believe that will be the duration of her stint in advertising.

"If you wish, we could arrange, so to speak, for a few unexpected difficulties to arise. Problems of too great an importance for Hudson to deal with alone. By doing so, we might be able to cause Mel to tire of the ownership idea sooner than she would otherwise."

"Now you're talking," laughed Suzanne, having about given up hope for her brother, who was becoming much too acquiescent of late. It was nice to see the old, devious Donald back.

"By the way, Sis, what did you mean when you wanted to know whom would receive ownership of the company, in the unlikely event of something happening to Melissa? Surely you are not thinking of doing anything stupid."

"Of course not. I just wondered, that's all." Donald was unconvinced by his sister's denial.

The Sunset View Inn was as delightful as Raymond had depicted. As its title implied, it offered a picturesque view overlooking a body of water which caught the fading rays of the sun, as it retired for the night.

Mrs. Wilson, the proprietress, was a pleasant, slightly corpulent lady in her mid-fifties. "I'm sure you will be very comfortable here," she said, as she proceeded to rave over the inn's many attractions. While escorting the young lady to her room, Mrs. Wilson tactfully asked a few personal questions. Questions designed to gain some insight into the personality of her new tenant.

The room Mel was assigned provided the luxury of a large picture window that fully captured the panorama for which the inn was aptly named.

"The inn is charming. I'm convinced my stay will be a memorable one." Melissa was not equipped with a crystal ball to warn her of the accuracy in her prophetic statement.

"We have a small dining room with a varied menu. Meal times are posted on the door of your room. Don't hesitate to inform me of any special requests or needs while you are with us."

"Thank you." Melissa appreciated the woman's efforts to make her feel at home.

"Would you be interested in our daily or weekly rates?"

"Weekly," responded Melissa. "My stay promises to be an extended one."

"Fine. Once you get settled, come to the office and we can negotiate a payment schedule. As a matter of fact, if you think the duration of your visit will be long enough to benefit from it, we could discuss a monthly fee. It would cost you less, in the end." Mrs. Wilson was impressed by the young nurse, with her fresh look and ingratiating personality, satisfied that she would be a welcome addition around the place.

"That would suit my needs perfectly." Melissa recognized, with the way things were shaping up, her tab for accommodations was in danger of adding up.

Melissa had notified her employer of her need for an indeterminate leave of absence, with an accompanying explanation as to what had transpired requiring alteration of her plans. Her request had been granted, with the understanding that she was to inform them of the specific time frame needed to fulfill her obligations, once those details became clear.

When her unpacking was complete, Melissa picked up the phone and dialed a number she had carefully memorized. In response to the third ring a male voice answered, "Hello."

"Everything seems to be going as planned. Is the situation copacetic at the other end?"

"It appears to be stable. For now. Let's hope it stays that way."

"With the instructions I received from Judith, and help from Mr. Hudson, I should be able to manage effectively in my new role.

"Donald and Suzanne can hardly oppose my appointment if I provide no basis for a valid complaint."

"It would be best not to appear too knowledgeable in the company's affairs. We do not want to create suspicion. Remember, a C.C.U. nurse would have little exposure to the advertising field. Be careful to act accordingly."

"Of course. I will take care to perform like the greenhorn they think I am."

"That would be best," her accomplice agreed. "Your cousins may be more observant than we are giving them credit for. We must also avoid further communication, if at all possible. Should our deception be uncovered, our goose, as the expression goes, is cooked."

"Definitely. Hopefully our scheme will progress without a hitch, thus removing any cause for discussion until our assignment is successfully brought to a close. God, I sound like an undercover agent, but, I guess that is what I am for now. Take care." Melissa signed off.

A similar conversation was being conducted elsewhere, also via the airwaves. The call originated from the mansion and involved members of both sexes.

"Melissa inherited the agency. I cannot believe that Mother let me down. She promised me the company. What do you propose we do now? Melissa has no experience. She will drive it into the ground in no time." The female voice was agitated, with an undercurrent of fear.

"It will be up to us to see that she does not get a chance to do so," the man countered.

"Just what do you mean by that?" The fear in the woman's tone was, justifiably, increased. She was no stranger to the violent potential latent in the man, having been on the receiving end of it in the past.

"Simply that we will do what is necessary to gain control of the agency. It was, after all, promised to you. Therefore, indirectly promised to me. Disappointment is not something I find appealing. I have worked for five years for that company, taking orders from other people. Waiting for the day when it would be my turn to run things and have people answer to me. That time is now. We have burned too many bridges to turn back."

"I feel the same way. Watching others receive the glory, when you know you are the one who deserves the praise. It is just that the idea of murder is repulsive to me."

"Drastic measures, such as elimination of the obstacle, are only used as a last resort. We will try other means of persuasion first. Just remember, whatever happens, we are in this together. If you chicken out on me now, you will live to regret it."

"I won't. We both want the same thing." The woman heard a noise in the hall. "Someone is coming. I had better go." She promptly ended the conversation. Calling her fellow conspirator was a risk not advisable to attempt on a regular basis. Due to the news revealed by the will, this conversation was unavoidable. It was urgent she inform him of the contents of the will, in an effort to establish a course of action. With the interruption causing her to break off contact, she was left in the dark as to what direction he wished to pursue. She had no option other than to follow his lead, until such time as his plans became clear.

Her most important task had been to dispose of the evidence. That she had done.

So obliging of Conrad to mention the problem he had been experiencing with rats in the stables. That had given her the idea of using the rat poison. The empty can, if discovered, would hardly be significant. It would be assumed that Conrad had used it to eliminate his problem. As she had used it, to eliminate her own.

And to think she had taken such care to administer the poison gradually, thus eliminating fear of the drug being detected through a blood test. Now, other means would have to be used to attain their goal. It would have been so much simpler if her mother had just kept her promise. Had she done so, further violence would have been unnecessary.

The fact that Judith had left the agency to Melissa had definitely put a snag in the works for several individuals. No one had remotely considered this possibility. Due to that oversight, their expectations would require serious alteration.

9

The following day began with Melissa's arrival at Carson Agency, eager to start her education, prior to assuming the managerial role she had taken on. Her introductory duties included addressing employees at a general staff meeting.

An opening speech was made by Timothy Hudson. If the staff were bewildered by the identity of Mrs. Carson's successor, they wisely hid their astonishment. Following Timothy's preamble, Melissa took center stage.

"Aunt Judith was proud of this agency and its reputation for quality in advertising. A reputation she largely attributed to all of you. Carson Agency has advanced to a lucrative level of achievement, on an international scale. This is a position we intend to maintain and, with your assistance, build upon.

"Although I lack extensive experience in this field, I look forward to the challenge this opportunity presents for me."

Following the meeting, Melissa and Timothy engaged in a detailed discussion.

"You're a brave woman, Ms. Sommers, to consider such a radical career change. Perhaps you would have been wise to decline your aunt's generous offer." Distinguished looking in his business suit, while rugged and masculine in his demeanor, Melissa found the presence of the young man somewhat overwhelming.

"Obviously my aunt had a valid reason for her decision. She must have believed that, despite my inexperience, I could make a contribution. Because of the faith she has shown in my abilities, I feel compelled to try to meet her expectations.

"She was exceptionally pleased with your efforts, Mr. Hudson. I have no plans, immediate or otherwise, to modify your job description. The only noticeable deviation from what has been, to date, the norm, is that you will now be reporting to me."

"There is one other difference you have not alluded to, Ms. Sommers," commented Timothy.

"Really, and what might that be?" A slight blush appeared on Mel's cheeks.

"Interference from your cousins. With their mother's presence in the background, they knew better than to oppose my authority. With her removal from the scene, I gather, their attitude toward me will undergo a drastic change." Timothy appeared oblivious to the look of disappointment on Melissa's face. She had vainly hoped that he was referring to the initial chemistry between them, when he acknowledged that there would be a difference in his working relationship with her and the rapport he had enjoyed with his previous boss. Apparently, the attraction she had assumed was mutual, existed only in her imagination.

All business this fellow, she thought. Very well, so be it.

"We will cross that bridge when we come to it," Mel replied, referring to the subject of her cousins' possible meddling. "As much as they object to it, the fact remains: Judith left this agency to me. They will have to live with her decision. At least until the will is successfully contested."

"That may, very well, be true. They can, nonetheless, make life exceedingly uncomfortable for you. And, considering my position here, I will be caught in the crossfire."

"Mr. Hudson, first of all I prefer to be addressed as Mel, or Melissa, if you find Mel too informal. And I will refer to you as Timothy, if you have no objection. Now that we have that out of the way, we can deal with more important issues.

"I see you as a man who responds well to pressure and, when it comes to crossfire, knows how to bop and weave."

"To a degree that is true. Just remember, Ma'am, I ain't no Muhammad Ali, and Suzanne Carson ain't no Joe Frazier. In fact, if the truth be known, she makes Smokin' Joe look like a pussycat," chuckled Timothy.

"I'll remember, Timothy." Mel held out her hand. "Are you willing to help me continue where Judith left off?"

"It would be my pleasure to do so, Melissa." Timothy grasped her extended hand and gently shook it. "Now is as good a time as any to get started."

Mel's first day, on the job, passed quickly. The time was spent reviewing files of major clients and discussing various current ad campaigns. Melissa was amazed by the number of people involved in each project. All staff members made significant contributions to the success of each campaign and were handsomely compensated for their services.

Melissa noticed an overall sense of job satisfaction among the staff. An attitude she acknowledged to Timothy. "No wonder the agency has fared so well. These people appear to excel at their trade, showing pride in their accomplishments. No small feat among today's work force."

"Judith tolerated nothing less than the very best from every employee. She had a knack for weeding out the undesirable, instinctively knowing which personnel were here to work and which employees tended to do barely enough to get by. Not because of any lack of competence on their part.

Simply a case of sheer laziness and absence of ambition. Those type never lasted long."

"How do you keep up-to-date with the various projects currently in production?"

"Simple, really. I insist, as did Mrs. Carson, on detailed reports of the current campaigns being conducted by the account executives. Each has been instructed to supply daily summaries of their progress. After five years, my reputation is well-known throughout the agency. I imagine they have names they use to refer to me, not all of which are charitable, though most likely deserved. The most important thing is that I get results. So long as they keep up the standards set down, we get along fine."

Mel noticed the vast number of phone messages and inquiries Timothy dealt with personally. Matters, she felt, should have been competently taken care of by the separate account executives. Mel asked the man to explain the need for such persistent overseeing on his part.

"I like to be aware of what is going on in the various departments at all times. If there is a problem, for example a delay in production, I need to be informed. When a client has a major complaint, it is normally addressed to me. Especially if he is voicing a complaint about the way his campaign is being run by a particular account manager. Therefore, it is vital that I know about any existent delay or problem before he does.

"Basically, the account executives handle most of the difficulties that arise, merely advising me of the situation and their proposed remedies. I am ultimately responsible for the outcome. However, I will only interfere if I feel they are not handling the problem properly, or if I am dissatisfied with the speed with which they are getting things accomplished.

"I'm sure you noticed that most of the calls are very short. We now have it down to a science. I guess you could call it verbal shorthand."

"I'll say. I'm amazed you can keep it all straight."

"That is largely due to the memory enhancing courses I

took while in college. They taught me techniques to use when trying to remember many, unrelated, topics. I have found them very beneficial."

"That explains it."

Melissa found the day, though exhausting, both informative and interesting. Timothy was approachable, showing no outward indication of feeling threatened by her assumption of authority. She was unprepared for the vast array of events that one encountered in an average business day at an advertising agency. Melissa realized that it would take some time for her to feel equipped to cope, without the assistant manager's guidance.

Leaving the office at the end of the day, Melissa observed Suzanne conversing with a young man outside of the creative department. As she walked by them, their verbal exchange became subdued, their manner secretive. I wonder what that was all about? Melissa's suspicious nature was alerted. Maybe the man was married and they were carrying in an illicit affair. Melissa scolded herself. She realized she was jumping to conclusions in regard to something that was really none of her business, or so she mistakenly assumed.

Immediately upon her arrival at the inn, Mel decided to take a shower before advancing to the dining room. After supper, she thought, I will make it an early evening. As she was leaving her room the phone rang, the caller being Timothy Hudson.

"Hope I am not intruding. There is a matter we should discuss, preferably away from the office environment. Could I infringe on your privacy long enough to have a word with you? It is rather urgent." The young man sounded worried.

"Certainly, Timothy. I was just leaving to go to supper in the dining room here at the inn. Why don't you join me? We can speak in relative seclusion here."

"That will be fine. I will be there in twenty minutes."

"Meet me in the lobby."

"Fine."

Melissa's mind was racing. What could be important

enough to prompt the assistant manager to request a conference this evening?

Deciding it was best to wait for the man to reveal the reason for the meeting, rather than invent any number of scenarios, Mel contemplated a change of attire.

Rarely did Melissa have cause to worry about her appearance. Routinely, her looks were something she paid little attention to. Unlike her cousin, she had never relied on her exterior presentation to gain acceptance or impress others. Cultivating a pleasing personality had been, to her, more important than spending countless hours preening in front of a mirror.

Tonight her honorable priorities went out the window. She found herself looking at her reflected image in a totally different light. The face looking back at her from the mirror was, suddenly, all wrong. Her nose was too big, her lips too small. Her eyes appeared crooked and disproportioned with the remaining features.

Once she transferred her field of vision to the trunk portion of her body she became despondent. What, up till now, had been adequate, suddenly became unacceptable. My God, she thought, Suzanne has taken up residence in my mind. Her cousin had always told her she should spend more time over her appearance. She had previously ignored Suzanne, rationalizing that she did not have extra time to waste toiling over her personal grooming. Ironically, she was now discovering that she regretted not having taken the woman's advice. A fact that she would never admit, even at gunpoint, to Suzanne.

"Well," Mel spoke aloud, "enough of this self-criticism. I must not keep Timothy waiting. I'll just have to make the best of what I have going for me and get to the lobby. After all, one can hardly consider this a date. The man simply wants to talk with me about a problem, no doubt related to our work situation."

An unbiased observer would have difficulty understanding Melissa's dissatisfaction. Their eyes would view a very attractive lady, not equipped with the stunning good looks of a fashion model, but no area of which she should feel ashamed. Her long flowing brunette hair had the sheen of healthiness, as did her complexion. Her figure, while not without flaws (what normal woman's body is absent of a few minor imperfections), was appealing. Many people would describe her as an exuberant, self-confident young woman.

Melissa's best feature (one which she failed to be conscious of) was her cheerful, engaging smile. A smile which proved to be contagious.

Suzanne, by far the more physically attractive female, lacked the pleasing disposition Melissa was noted for.

Under normal circumstances, Melissa would agree that the interior was far more important than the exterior anyway. As far as people were concerned. But, with her desire to impress Timothy Hudson, the current circumstances could hardly be considered normal.

Melissa opted for casual attire, selecting blue jeans and a loose fitting sweater. Anything more elegant would be inappropriate for the inn's dining room. She did not wish to look out of place, which would draw attention to herself and make her dinner companion ill at ease. When Mel became better acquainted with the assistant manager, she would come to the realization that he was a man unimpressed by finery and unnatural beauty. He preferred a woman who was self-assured and accepted her own body, imperfections and all. His initial impression of Melissa had been that of a female who fit his ideal. A pleasant change from the bevy of beauties normally vying for his attention.

10

Timothy arrived in exactly twenty minutes, adding punctuality to the list of attributes Melissa was comprising to describe him. Clad in blue jeans and a plaid shirt, Melissa again found herself drawn to his pleasant features. Evidently she had followed her better instincts in choosing casual dress.

Timothy was not unmoved by the attractiveness of his new boss. At the moment, however, he felt it wise to pursue a purely professional relationship. Mixing business with pleasure seldom worked satisfactorily, in his experience. One of the two usually suffered. Mr. Hudson enjoyed his present position with the agency and had no desire to do anything which might jeopardize his job situation. He found Ms. Sommers to be a nice lady, with similar traits as that of her predecessor. But, despite the existent chemistry between them (chemistry he sensed Mel was cognizant of), Timothy elected to maintain an arm's length approach. A resolution, he admitted, would not be easy to keep.

As they said their hellos, they entered the dining room and located a corner table which afforded the most privacy. A waiter promptly took their orders and left them to their discussion.

"I hope I did not alarm you, Melissa," Timothy initiated the conversation. "That was not my intention. It is just that a problem has arisen in the accounting department, which I felt you should be made aware of. For awhile now, we have noticed some selective discrepancies. In the beginning the differences were slight. But, lately, there have been larger variances noted."

"What exactly do you mean?" asked Mel.

"For example, yesterday Mr. Allen called me. He is the general manager of one of our client companies. A company we have been doing business with for several years. He was asking about the recent increase in our rates."

"Let me guess," volunteered Mel, "the rates have remained unchanged."

"No, they have changed. Just not to the degree Mr. Allen received notification of. With the inflated price of supplies and increased production costs, we have been forced to transfer a percentage of our escalating expenses to our customers. The problem is: the sum Mr. Allen quoted is a good deal higher than a normal price hike."

"Have you been able to discover how the error occurred?"

"Not as yet. I assured Allen that I would look into the matter, without delay. When I checked with our accounting department, their records show that the amount received was an appropriate charge. We have no record of the figure Allen states he was billed for."

"Have there been other complaints of this nature?"

"No. This is the first. The previous discrepancies involved expenditures."

"Do you have any idea who is responsible for these inconsistencies?"

"No. The chief accountant has been with the agency longer than myself. To my knowledge, there has never been any hint of impropriety on his part. He is, understandably, upset over the whole affair."

Mel was not anxious to deal with as serious an issue as embezzlement so soon after starting her new assignment. Despite her misgivings, however, she knew it was a predicament that required an immediate and detailed investigation. "How many people have direct access to the accounting department or to the ledgers and official billing documents?" she asked Timothy.

"There are four people employed in the accounting department, not including Simon Jennings, the chief accountant. Jennings rechecks all incoming and outgoing data daily. Photocopies are then sent to Donald or Suzanne, for verification and review."

"When were you first made aware of any difficulties?"

"Approximately six months ago. Money was allocated to the stores department for supplies which were never ordered, nor received. When Jennings advised me of his findings, I approached your cousins in regard to the matter. They claimed ignorance, but promised they would familiarize themselves with the problem immediately. After I learned of their hesitation in doing so, I informed Mrs. Carson of Simon's discovery, in order to establish how she wished to deal with the issue. She instructed me to leave the matter with her, guaranteeing her prompt attention to the situation. Shortly after she learned of the problem, there was no further indication of any irregularity. Not that is, until now."

"The method employed on this occasion is quite different from that previously used. Apparently a more ingenious plan if it escaped Mr. Jennings watchful eye," noted Mel.

"Yes. As far as I can tell, Mr. Allen's company paid the sum which had been stipulated when the contract was signed. Within a few days after submitting this payment, they received a bill requiring an additional premium for unexpected expenses incurred. It was this amount which was deposited elsewhere."

"I gather we have prearranged rates which are clearly delineated."

"Precisely. The estimated costs are laid out prior to the service contract. The contract does specify that variations to the final amount payable can be made, within very specific guidelines. People whom we rely on for supplies and other necessities, at times jack their prices without much notice. Contracts our clients sign must reflect these unexpected increases. If not, we stand to lose a substantial amount of money. We must maintain a specific margin of profit. Failing that, we would very quickly be unable to meet our financial obligations, not the least of which being salaries."

"Did Mr. Allen say from whom he received notification of the change in costs?"

"That is where it gets sticky. He states he received a letter from our accounting department, requesting the additional sum. The letter clearly displayed our letterhead. What is even more incriminating, is the presence of Simon Jennings' signature."

"Can we get a copy of that letter?" requested Mel.

"I am to meet with Mr. Allen tomorrow. He has promised to bring the official letter, a copy of which he has made for his own records. Perhaps you would care to join me at that meeting?"

"Most definitely. I suggest that Simon Jennings also attend, since it is his integrity that is under attack."

"Good idea. He is eager to get this thing settled and prove he is innocent of any wrongdoing."

"Do you think Donald and Suzanne are somehow involved in this scheme?" Melissa verbalized the question which was impossible to ignore.

"I really can't say. When the original discrepancies took place, it was their responsibility to double check Jennings' figures. They gave no indication of noticing any abnormality.

When Simon failed to get a response from the report outlining the contradictions, he went to see them. At that time they appeared, by Simon's interpretation, unconcerned over the situation, making no effort to rectify the error. Nor did they instigate an inquiry into a possible case of embezzlement. Of course, we will need more proof before making any accusations implying their involvement."

"Was there any chance they had been subtly looking into the matter and were simply unable to come up with any explanation for the falsified orders, or discover who was responsible?" Melissa wished to give her cousins the benefit of a doubt, though only if deserved. If, indeed, they had been instrumental in their mother's poisoning, taking part in an embezzlement plot paled in comparison. Had they been stealing money from the company and Judith accused them of the offense, that would create another motive for murder.

"Anything is possible. That is why I attempted to find out if they had begun some form of investigation into the cause of the conflicting reports. No employee could recall being questioned on the topic, or knew of any interrogation. If someone was, even discreetly, asking questions of the nature necessary to flush out an embezzler, it is highly unlikely, in an agency of this size, that the news would fail to leak out.

"It was only after verifying their lack of progress that I consulted Mrs. Carson. With the cessation of the illegal activities, I naturally assumed the problem had been effectively solved. She did not report to me in regard to the matter and I did not feel it was my place to broach the subject with her. Nor did I wish to create any embarrassment for her, given the possibility that her children had been mixed up in the scheme.

"When this latest situation arose, I saw little point in conferring with Donald or Suzanne, based on the previous episode. As you had just started, I contemplated sparing you the aggravation. Ultimately, I decided that was not my call to make."

"No matter how much I would like to," responded Melissa, "I can't avoid unpleasant situations just because I am the new kid on the block. I took on this assignment, fully realizing that problems were apt to arise, though I will admit, I had hoped for a longer reprieve. Nonetheless, I am prepared to take the good with the bad."

"Once we have spoken with Mr. Allen we will have more to go on. With any luck, that will help decide our course of action. I am confident we can gain control of this predicament before it mushrooms."

"I'm glad that you feel so assured." Melissa clearly lacked the degree of certainty that Timothy possessed. "I will follow your lead and trust your judgment as to the best path to travel. These people know you. They feel comfortable with you. You're not the stranger who has taken over the agency. They feel no affiliation with me. Even Donald and Suzanne are less likely to open up to me than they will to you. After all, you pose no threat to them. You're not the good-for-nothing relative who stole the agency out from under them. An achievement hardly worthy of undying affection."

Conversation continued over dinner, with the subject matter taking a much lighter vein. The two discussed childhood memories, education and the motivating factors behind their career choices.

"Nursing was a way to make a contribution. I admit that sounds corny but it was my incentive at the time. I was much younger then and thought I could change the world."

"Don't we all?" interjected Timothy.

"We do when we start out. The nursing profession has undergone many alterations over the years. Some beneficial, though many have been regressive. Lately I have found myself doing a fair bit of soul searching as to whether or not it is the career I wish to continue pursuing. The common term for the turmoil going on inside me is 'burnout', though I am not convinced my dissatisfaction has reached that level. As a result of Judith's passing, I have been given an opportunity to actively survey other options. Not many people get that chance. It is regrettable that it has come as a result of such misfortune." Melissa spoke frankly.

"You were very close to your aunt." Timothy observed the sadness in Mel's features.

"She was like a second mother to me. I will miss her dreadfully." Melissa's voice was thick with emotion. "Anyway, enough about me. What was the driving force prompting you to enter the field of advertising?"

"I've always been intrigued by the notion of being amid the movers and shakers. I'm essentially power hungry." Mel spotted the mischievous twinkle in the young man's eye. "Art has been a passion of mine since early childhood. I feel that good advertising is an art form, one which welds a lot of power. The basic consumer, despite his or her denials, responds to advertising. They may complain about the number of commercials which disrupt their favorite movie or television show, but statistics reveal that the average shopper consistently purchases products they are familiar with. Knowledge that comes, primarily, as a result of those advertisements they constantly complain about.

"People are less likely to buy articles foreign to them. In fact, consumers are the best advertisers. For example, if they have tried a product and been pleased with its results, it is an absolute certainty that they will tell their friends. Those friends tell others and so the circle continues. Our job is to be the catalyst that starts the chain reaction." Timothy spoke, zealously, on the topic which was close to his heart.

"You obviously love your work. I gather burnout poses no threat to your mental attitude."

"No, I see no hint of it in the immediate future. I still find the work rewarding, both monetarily and creatively."

The two diners enjoyed the delectable meal, following their main course selections with coffee and cheesecake.

"Are you an only child?" inquired Mel, wishing to learn more about her dinner companion.

"Sometimes I wish." Timothy chuckled. "I have three brothers and two sisters. They are quite the crew, believe me. Sometimes I wonder how my parents managed to survive our upbringing, with any semblance of sanity remaining."

"I'm sure they loved every minute of it."

"You haven't met my siblings. Your opinion may change drastically, should that opportunity present itself."

"I look forward to the prospect," announced Melissa, certain that Timothy's view of his family was negatively biased.

"What about yourself? Are there any more Sommers?"

"Yes, as a matter of fact, there are six more in my family. Two boys and four girls. We get along as well as most large families. Aside from the normal sibling rivalry, which seems unavoidable."

"Yes, I guess that is part of the package."

Aside from the embezzlement predicament, the evening was pleasant for both parties. As they completed their conversation Melissa thanked the young man for confiding in her. Both expressed a sincere wish to find a rapid solution to the predicament currently facing Carson Agency.

11

On return to her room, Melissa debated contacting her associate to notify him of the agency dilemma. But, after much deliberation, she decided against it. Their agreement was to get in touch only under extreme circumstances. Although the present difficulty definitely qualified as extreme, Melissa felt the details were too sketchy to provide an accurate picture of the predicament. Following the meeting in the morning, Melissa would be better able to judge whether or not she was equipped to handle the crisis alone. Or, for that matter, if she wanted to. Needless to say, this type of scenario had not been discussed. It would be a judgment call. One she would have to make quickly.

The moment Mel settled herself into the comfortable

lounger (a focal point of her temporary home), fatigue made its presence felt. She was aware that sleep was essential, if she were to be well rested for the conference. With this objective in mind, she performed her nightly ritual and retired.

A night of uninterrupted slumber was a hoped for luxury she was not to be afforded. Leastwise, not tonight. The incessant pealing of the phone awoke her abruptly from sleep. Her initial greeting was met with silence. A repeat of her "Hello," again received no verbal reply. Irritated by the lack of response, she spoke angrily, "If you have the audacity to call someone in the middle of the night, the least you can do is talk." With this, she slammed the receiver into its cradle.

After this experience Mel was disturbed to notice herself trembling. The young woman, adept at coping with unwelcome events, was surprised by her uncharacteristic reaction. Quickly reasoning that her response to the call was due to the lateness of the hour and the fact that she had been woken from a deep sleep, Mel tried to analyze the unexpected intrusion.

Few people knew she was residing at the inn. Those who did, were hardly the type to harass her in this fashion. Even Donald and Suzanne were unlikely candidates. Really, could one picture Suzanne disrupting her beauty sleep to make a phone call. Especially one where she didn't utter a word. Not on your life!

The only logical explanation was that the caller was attempting to reach the former occupant of the room. When an unrecognizable voice answered, the caller was caught off guard, not knowing what to say. With this rationale firmly implanted, Melissa returned to bed, certain she had solved the mystery.

When a similar episode occurred, twice more, before dawn, Mel was not as convinced of the accuracy of her assessment of the caller's motivation. Due to these further impingements on her right to a restful night, the young woman was tired and exasperated when morning arrived. Despite a hot, lengthy shower, she remained less than exuberant as she headed to the office.

Timothy noticed, and quickly commented on, the fatigue evident on Mel's features. In answer to his inquiry as to the cause for her obvious lack of sleep (expressing his concern that their discussion had contributed to her restlessness), she recounted the episodes which had interfered with her slumber.

"Do you have any idea who it was?" Timothy asked, obviously concerned for her safety.

"At first I thought perhaps it was a wrong number and the caller was too embarrassed to admit it. That has been known to happen. Or maybe they were surprised to hear a woman's voice on the line, the former occupant being a man. I disregarded both of those theories, however, after the second call."

"It was probably someone not pleased with your new acquisition. Perhaps they were afraid you would recognize their voice, were they to speak. If they remained silent, their aim of harassment could be accomplished without danger of being identified.

"You should notify the phone company. Ask them to put a tap on the phone, in case the person calls again."

"I will check into that."

"Do you feel up to attending this meeting? I can go alone, if you prefer."

"No, I'll be fine. The best way to learn about a company is to participate in its activities. Besides, it is possible that this embezzlement business is somehow tied in with Judith's murder. If so, the sooner we find out who is responsible, the closer we come to solving the identity of her assailant. Judith was aware of the first occurrence and told you she would look into it. Perhaps she did. By investigating the matter, she may have signed her own death warrant. The time frame is consistent to connect the two events. Embezzlement and a jail term, if caught, could make a person desperate enough to commit murder."

"If the two events are related, the finger of blame would point directly at your cousins, wouldn't it? They are the only ones with a link between the mansion and the agency. Haven't the police all but eliminated the possibility of Judith's murderer being an outsider?"

"Yes, the number of people potentially involved in both matters does not comprise a very long list. Donald and Suzanne had the best motive. Shortage of funds could explain the embezzlement attempt and their desire to lay their hands on their inheritance."

"I cannot imagine anyone killing their own mother for the sake of money. Nobody could be that desperate."

"I have some trouble with that one myself, but it does happen. If a person has always been able to obtain all their monetary wants and needs, then suddenly are faced with the loss of that security, they could become desperate enough to commit such a crime. They may, afterward, feel remorse over what they did, while still able to justify their action."

"It is amazing what our minds can make us believe is acceptable conduct," remarked Timothy.

"What is equally difficult to grasp is how they can brainwash others into accepting their rationale. They can convince some people that their action was unavoidable and warranted. Pretty scary."

"I suppose, in reality, that is a version of the method used by anyone trying to sell an idea. Advertisers being no exception. We do the talking. It is up to the listener to decide if they wish to believe what they are hearing."

"Basically, the outcome is similar. There is a positive and negative side to everything."

"That is the primary reason why Judith refused to accept clients whose product she was not impressed with. People can be gullible at times. A human being's instincts are to trust others, until such time as they no longer deserve that trust. There are individuals in society who depend on these fundamental instincts. Using them, to their advantage. Judith would never be party to such conduct. Any product we advertise is as good, if not better, than our ads state. There are laws protecting consumers against false claims by advertisers. Because of these, manufacturers must be very cautious not to promote false expectations among their customers. Some people have unrealistic expectations in regard to the successful application of certain products but, usually, the consumer is responsible for their own attitude in this regard. If they feel they have a legitimate complaint, there are avenues they can pursue to voice their objection."

Fortified, after ingesting her third cup of coffee, not a frequent indulgence for Melissa, she felt reasonably prepared to attend the meeting with Mr. Allen.

Seymour Allen, normally an amiable man, was not in a pleasant frame of mind this morning. A presentation which, while Mel could understand, did nothing to ease her troubled mind. Timothy had supplied a detailed account of the agency's business dealings with Mr. Allen's company. A relationship that, to date, had been satisfactory and mutually profitable. Mr. Allen had never voiced complaints in regard to the management of his advertising account, often remarking on how honestly and efficiently Carson Agency was directed. So much so that several new clients had been secured, based on the man's recommendation.

Allen attributed the recent difficulties to the absence of Mrs. Carson, a woman he had admired for her ability to run a tight ship. She had kept a close eye on all that transpired in her organization. Considering the clientele it was rumored the agency could boast, that was not an accomplishment to be taken lightly. With her absence, someone must have seized on this vulnerable time of change to relieve the agency of some of its funds. The realization that his company was to be one of the avenues by which such a procedure was undertaken, did not sit well with the businessman.

Preliminary introductions taken care of, Seymour Allen presented the letter which he had received requesting the additional payment. Clearly displayed across the bottom of the stationary was what appeared to be the signature of Simon Jennings, head accountant of Carson Agency.

"Is this your signature?" Melissa addressed the man in question.

"It sure looks like my writing. Here, see for yourself." Simon scrawled his name on a scratch pad, handing it to Mel.

"There isn't much doubt that the resemblance is striking." Mel pointed out, while passing it to those positioned around the conference table. "The only way to verify its authenticity is through consultation with a handwriting expert."

"I swear," Mr. Jennings was distraught and made no effort to conceal his emotions, "I do not remember signing that letter."

"I believe you, Simon." Timothy verbalized his faith in the accountant. During his five-year acquaintance with the man, Timothy could not recall any prior display of emotion. Not that he lacked just cause for an indication of dissatisfaction. No doubt there had been several occasions when Simon was seething inside. After all, the man's job description dictated frequent contact with Suzanne Carson.

Timothy remembered more than one individual remarking on what an even-tempered man Simon was. Judith herself had often asked Timothy if the head accountant expressed any hint of discontentment with his station. If Simon was disgruntled, he kept it to himself. Timothy had not been privy to any rumors of Simon's dissatisfaction and the man had never approached him with a complaint of that nature.

The reason for Simon's normally unimpassioned presentation was largely due to his upbringing. His father, a restrained man, tolerated no emotional display from his wife or children in his presence. When he was absent, Simon's mother had made a special effort to encourage free expression from her offspring. She advised them to reserve any outward display of disappointment or excitement, for such times. Fortunately, Mr. Jennings' occupation required extensive travel. Therefore, the time for restraint was seldom prolonged.

The main cause for Simon's failure to complain or engage in any displays of temper was that he was, generally, satisfied with both his personal and professional life. He had a lovely wife and three children, of whom he was tremendously proud and with whom he did not hesitate to show his affection.

With maturity, came the realization that not all of what his father had tried to instill in him was unhealthy. The aim of keeping one's negative emotions in check, to a degree, is wise. He had learned, however, as a result of his mother's thoughtful teachings, that there was a time when it was prudent to let people know how one felt. Be it by exhibiting signs of love and caring, or through a show of annoyance (if necessary to get one's point across).

Simon restricted his displays of irritation to isolated, verbal outbursts. The small contingent of people who had been recipients of his temper cautioned others not to provide sufficient provocation to incite him.

There was one other reason for Simon's refusal to complain about his work situation. He worshipped the ground Mrs. Carson had walked on. Simon had loved the woman almost as much as he loved his own wife, though in the purest sense of the word. He had felt no romantic inclination toward her. Simon had loved her as a person. One of the most beautiful souls he had ever encountered. This was an opinion shared by Mrs. Jennings.

How many bosses would open their heart and home to an employee and his family when that man had lost everything, including a small child, in a house fire? Mrs. Carson had helped them get back on their feet, both financially and emotionally. By verbalizing dissatisfaction with any aspect of his employment, Simon felt he would be offending Mrs. Carson. That was something he could never do.

In actuality, the only complaint Simon had was in regard to the total incompetence of Judith's daughter. In his opinion, if the initial problem had been addressed when he first informed Suzanne of his findings, today's meeting would have been unnecessary. Simon's appraisal of Suzanne (an appraisal shared by others), assessed her as lacking qualities essential in a person occupying the position of authority she held. She was incapable of setting priorities, her main concern being her social calendar. Simon realized he should have taken the information about the bogus stock orders to Mr. Hudson sooner than he had. He might have known that Suzanne would dig her heels in if she did not feel the matter warranted her immediate attention. What would qualify, in her estimation, as a circumstance requiring her to forego her personal activities, were facts known only to herself.

"Is there any chance you signed the letter in haste, without checking it thoroughly?" asked Timothy.

"Any financial arrangements which deviate from established guidelines are to be cleared through me, or by way of Mr. or Ms. Carson. All employees are aware of this requirement and strictly adhere to it. It is their responsibility to ensure that anything of that nature is presented for our approval. No one working in the accounting department would place a document of such importance on my desk without verifying my knowledge of its presence.

"Even if, by chance, they had neglected to ensure my awareness of the paper I, habitually, check every form I put my signature to. It is irresponsible to sign one's name to a document without being certain of its contents. One thing I have never been accused of is irresponsibility."

"I did not mean to imply that you were irresponsible," stated Timothy, by way of apology. "But there are occasions, when one becomes busy, that forms are passed over quickly."

"Mr. Allen," Melissa addressed the businessman. "I promise that we will begin a thorough investigation immediately. You will be reimbursed for the sum you were billed, with interest. Being a valued customer, we have no desire to alienate you. However, it is pointless to make false promises. Rest assured, we will endeavor to see that such an episode is not repeated. I politely request you to inform us of any further irregularities, should they occur without our knowledge. Being a businessman yourself, you know that these situations occur. It has been my experience that the solution to such a problem rarely comes speedily. We hope you will bear with us, until we can find that solution." Melissa had always found the idea of sugarcoating a problem revolting and without merit. As no possible benefit would be derived from downplaying the circumstance, she exercised a forthright approach.

"You are a lot like your aunt, Ms. Sommers," said Mr.

Allen. Considering his exalted opinion of Judith, this was high praise indeed. "Mrs. Carson was never one to beat around the bush. If she had something to say, she said it. I like that in a business associate. That way I know where I stand. For now, I will make no changes in our working relationship. I have never had reason for concern before. One little hint of trouble is not enough to make me forget all the years of reliable service we have received from this agency. As you say, these things happen to the best of companies. I, too, have been in the middle of a similar situation. For your sake, I hope this situation meets as satisfactory an outcome as I was able to attain." Handshakes signified the close of the meeting, Mr. Allen and his delegates departed.

"What did he mean by that?" asked Melissa, confused by Allen's closing comment.

"Some years ago there were rumors of a case of embezzlement at the company where Mr. Allen was employed," explained Simon. "Ironically, Allen was the one accused of misappropriating funds. It took several months for the truth to come out. Ultimately they learned the owner's son was responsible. I wonder if this case will result in a similar conclusion."

"Let's hope, if it does, we arrive at that conclusion in less time than it took him."

"One thing in my favor is that I am not working alone to clear my name," responded Simon. "I am grateful that you have shown faith in me, despite having little to go on."

"With your work record, Simon, you deserve our trust," stated Timothy. "But, should we find that you have betrayed that trust, the results will not be pleasant for you." The assistant manager wanted his position made abundantly clear. He was basing his assumption of Simon's honesty on past performance. But he wanted the man to know that, had he deceived them, he would not get a second chance to do so.

"I expect nothing more," said Simon. "That is precisely what Mrs. Carson would have said. Your confidence in me is not misplaced. On that, you have my word."

"Your word is good enough for me, Simon," proclaimed Timothy.

"Simon, can you please explain, in more detail the incident with the bogus stock orders," requested Melissa.

"Approximately six months ago we had a couple of occasions when money was paid out, by way of the store room, for supplies we never received. When I checked into the orders, the stores department could not locate their copy of the purchase form requisitioning the materials. Normally, both the accounting department and the stores department keep a copy of all order forms. We have our copy, theirs is nowhere to be found. The only way supplies can be purchased is with such a form."

"That appears to be a fairly impenetrable system," commented Mel.

"We had, up to that time, found it extremely efficient. With the large volume of supplies necessary to run an agency of this size, Mrs. Carson began the cross-reference method to maintain accurate records and avoid unnecessary overstocking. It also served as a deterrent, dissuading employees from removing articles from the company stock for personal use. A common occurrence prior to the application of this routine.

"Most requests for supplies are made to the stock room who place the orders. Upon receipt of the order, the forms are signed by the stock room attendant receiving the goods. Large wholesale orders are placed weekly, biweekly, or monthly, depending on usual demand. If the volume or frequencies of these orders change appreciably, it is my job to find out why.

"On those occasions I have spoken of, I noticed a sum of money delved out for supplies we normally order on a biweekly basis, the need for them being fairly consistent and predictable. A repeat order was placed within a week of the previous one."

"How could anyone think such a ruse could escape detection?" asked Melissa, confused as to why someone would attempt a plan with such strong probability of failure.

"You must understand. The articles ordered are items we

use extensively. Not many people would realize the normal requirement for the materials. Being a meticulous person, I have a keen eye for inconsistencies. When I see such a large order placed a week after those supplies were replenished, items whose use varies little, my alarm system becomes activated."

"Wouldn't the accountant that okayed the funds have questioned the need for the supplies?" asked Mel.

"That is not part of their job. Their responsibility is to insure that the proper purchase order form is present and appropriately signed. Most of our staff would not question the allotment of funds, if the necessary papers accompany the request.

"No system is perfect. Even when you think you have prevented all possible means of deception, someone is devious enough and intelligent enough to bypass the most complex controls."

"The form your department received requesting the extra funds was signed by whom?" This was Timothy's question.

"Mr. Dalton, head of the stores department. His signature was on both documents, the one denoting receipt of the goods and the form requesting the order."

"What was his response when faced with this evidence?"

"He was dumbfounded. Denied having been responsible for, or indeed having any knowledge of, the additional order. Supplies shown on the purchase requisition were materials he planned to replenish the following week, which would have been consistent with normal usage. We checked in every area of the stock room, to insure the goods had not simply been misplaced. There was no indication that the supplies had arrived. A call to the wholesalers verified no receipt of goods, as they denied having received the order."

"What of the signature? Did Mr. Dalton deny that as well?"

"Yes and no. He admitted that it closely resembled his handwriting, but denies signing the paper."

"It appears that, not only do we have a thief in our midst,

we also have an excellent forger. Based on the assumption that both Jennings' and Dalton's signatures were falsified by the same hand." Timothy suggested the only logical explanation, if they were to believe in the innocence of both men.

"So it would seem," agreed Melissa.

"You employed a rather daring approach with the distinguished Mr. Allen," teased the young man.

"I gather you would have used a more orthodox style."

"Probably, though I'm certain my efforts would have been dismally less productive. You impressed him with your candor and honesty. Not the accepted way of doing things, especially the candor. But, as my father says, 'If something works, don't knock it.'

"Your resemblance to your aunt may, in part, account for Seymour's reaction to you."

"I prefer to make my own way, on my own merits, Mr. Hudson." Melissa was slightly annoyed by Timothy's remark.

"I did not mean to offend. It is just that, in business, clients like to see consistency. When Mrs. Carson passed away, I'm sure many of our clients believed the agency would be poorly controlled without her at the helm. They have had some dealings with your cousins, you understand, causing them to fear the worst. Your appearance will set them on their collective ears. That will be rather pleasant.

"A warning, though. Try not to expect too much of yourself. That type of attitude can be dangerous."

12

"Where do we go from here?" asked Simon.

"I think we can safely assume that both cases are connected," replied Mel. "No doubt instigated by the same person, or persons. A warning from Judith may have prompted them to temporarily cease their illegal venture. Once she was out of the way, an event they may have participated in, they felt it was safe to resume their caper. To prevent repeat detection, they settled on a new plan. One they believed was superior to their previous method. If we go with these assumptions, I feel it is wise to check into both situations simultaneously.

"First, we should find out which of Simon's associates received and approved the false order form. They may be able to remember who presented the document to them."

"We have a slight problem there, Ms. Sommers. We have an in-house messenger service who are responsible for all internal and outgoing mail deliveries."

"Right, I forgot about that." Melissa acknowledged her momentary memory lapse.

"Just a second," said Timothy. "We could check with the messenger who made mail deliveries to the fifth floor on the day in question. He may recall who summoned him to the stores department to deliver the form."

"It is worth a try," agreed Simon. "Though I have my doubts any messenger would remember a particular order placed six months ago."

"Could one of you please tell me what you are talking about?" requested Mel, feeling left out of the conversation.

"Sorry," said Timothy, and began to explain facts only the two gentlemen were cognizant of. "One messenger is assigned to deliver all correspondence to a particular floor each day. The schedule is kept for several months. If an item was supposed to have arrived on a designated floor, on a specific day, and was mislaid we can discover, by reviewing the schedule, the messenger responsible. We can use the same system to recheck who was making deliveries to the fifth floor on the day the bogus purchase order arrived in accounting."

"Excellent," Melissa joined in the enthusiasm. "Timothy, why don't you check into that?"

"Right away, Captain." Timothy saluted in a humorous fashion.

"There is one more point I find confusing," stated Mel.

"Yes, Miss," responded Simon.

"Why is it necessary for the form to be brought to your department for allocation of funds? Why wouldn't Mr. Dalton simply write a check to the suppliers?"

"We used to employ that method. Mrs. Carson decided it was easier to maintain an accurate account of finances if all funds were dispensed from a central location. If there was any question in regard to the amounts requested, we were instructed to contact either her or Mr. Hudson. It was up to them to accept or deny the request."

"As you previously stated, if the purchase order forms were present, with necessary signatures in place, they usually escaped further scrutiny?"

"Yes. We have several forms arriving in our department every day. If we stopped and checked every one with a fine-toothed comb, we would fail to get any other work accomplished. Only a document lacking proper signature, or application for an unreasonable amount, underwent closer perusal."

"Do we pay the wholesalers by company check?"

"Yes. In this case, the check was made out to Goodman's Wholesalers. It was cashed, though no one at the wholesalers admits to receiving it." Simon supplied the details.

"Does the canceled check bear the company stamp of the wholesalers on it?"

"Yes, that is the only way their checks can be cashed."

"Apparently our culprit has contacts outside of this agency who are helping him in his scheme. That is the only explanation for him getting his hands on the wholesalers' stamp."

"That would be easy enough to do. Perhaps he knew someone who worked for the wholesalers and paid him a tidy sum to confiscate a stamp pad with their logo on it," suggested Simon.

"How many times did this type of false ordering take place?" asked Mel.

"There were three occasions that I know of. When the first one occurred, I assumed that, for some unaccountable reason, we had exceeded our customary use of the materials specified. I was not particularly disturbed by this, as it does happen from time to time. When we have new staff in the store room who are unfamiliar with the normal requirement, they have a tendency to overstock.

"After it happened twice more, in rapid succession, I thought it wise to investigate. That was when I approached Mr. Dalton. There may have been previous falsified orders, but those are the only ones I am aware of. I think they had been engaged in the activity for a while before it came to my attention. The more success they had, the bolder they became, eventually increasing the frequency of their operation. If they had not done so, it is difficult to say how long they could have continued with no one the wiser.

"After sounding out Mr. Dalton I submitted a detailed written report to Suzanne Carson. I was surprised when she did not contact me in regard to the matter, but thought perhaps she had looked into the situation through alternate channels, assuming that I had given all the information I could on the subject. When I discovered no evidence of this being the case, I paid a visit to her office. I prefer to deal with Mr. Carson, but he was unavailable and I did not wish to put the situation off any longer.

"When I voiced my concerns to Ms. Carson, reminding her that I had clearly outlined similar facts in the report I had submitted five days previous, she told me she had been too busy to read my submission. She promised she would do so immediately and take appropriate action."

"Why would you not go to Mr. Hudson with such a grave matter?"

"Mrs. Carson instructed all employees to deal with any irregularity, by way of the proper managerial channels. Mr. and Ms. Carson are my immediate superiors. Any difficulty I experienced was to be directed toward them. I followed proper protocol by speaking with Ms. Carson, after she had obviously ignored my written documentation of events." Simon stated his case matter-of-factly and confidently, knowing his action had been appropriate.

"It is apparent, Mr. Jennings, that you did everything within your power to inform management that a problem existed. This company should be thankful for your 'alarm system', without which this scheme would not have been brought to light as quickly as it was."

"Thank you, Miss." Simon was relieved that Ms. Sommers did not hold him responsible for the delay in investigating the previous embezzlement situation.

"I want to know why Suzanne hesitated in checking into these fictitious orders. I also would be interested in learning if Donald shared his sister's knowledge and, too, chose to ignore the matter." Melissa sensed a showdown with her cousins was due.

"Although Simon spoke only with Suzanne, I approached both of your cousins when I learned of the problem," stated Timothy. "It is possible Donald was unaware of the matter until that time. He gives the impression of having a stronger sense of accountability than his sister.

"Perhaps we should be present when you speak with them. For backup." Timothy thought it unwise for Melissa to enter the lion's den, unaccompanied.

"Not a bad idea. I can use all the support I can get. After we finish with Donald and Suzanne, you should check into that messenger schedule you mentioned."

Melissa notified her cousins of her wish to speak with them. Although Suzanne attempted to postpone the meeting, Mel would have none of it. After providing the woman with a brief summary as to the reason for the conference, Mel announced, "Suzanne this is an important matter which cannot be put off. We expect you in the conference room within ten minutes."

Suzanne had other things on her mind. She had arranged a meeting of a different sort, to be conducted at a motel not far from the office. Her friend was not pleased when she had to cancel, but claimed to understand. Wednesday was his day off. The day they normally met early. No one missed Suzanne at the agency one morning a week. In fact, they were glad for the reprieve.

"I will leave work early this afternoon, instead. Meet me at the motel at three," said Suzanne.

"Don't keep me waiting. You know how I feel about waiting."

"Yes, I know."

Damn Melissa, thought her cousin. She is cramping my style already, and she has only been here two days.

13

After contacting Suzanne and Donald, Melissa informed the remaining members of the accounting staff of her wish to have them join the meeting, thirty minutes after her appointment with the others. Melissa had no desire to embarrass her cousin, by confronting them in front of employees they normally supervised. An action which was unnecessary and Melissa deemed unprofessional.

Mel's cousins arrived promptly, though neither of them seemed impressed with the impromptu meeting.

Faced with the possibility of defending himself against allegations of embezzlement, Donald appeared nervous. Suzanne, however, was her usual abrasive self.

"I fail to see why you thought it necessary to call this

meeting today. The problem with the extra stock orders has already been rectified, quite competently I might add." Suzanne's manner disguised any guilt one would assume she should be feeling, considering her inappropriate and delayed reaction to the predicament.

"Really, Ms. Carson," Timothy made no effort to disguise his disgust. "May I ask, if you handled the situation so competently, why you failed to inform me of the successful resolution to the dilemma? Must I remind you that, if it had not been for Mr. Jennings, I would have been totally ignorant of the whole affair?

"It is your responsibility to notify me of any circumstance you become aware of that either exceeds your authority or which you cannot effectively handle unassisted. Not only did you fail to confer with me in regard to this matter, you also left me in the dark as to what, if anything, you planned to do to rectify it. It was only after Jennings was given reason to believe you were dragging your heels that he approached me. A decision warranted by your delay."

"I told Mr. Jennings I would look into it and I had every intention of doing so. He simply did not allow me enough time before running to you." The hostility in Suzanne's tone matched Timothy's.

"Ms. Carson, it was a week after his discussion with you, which by the way was five days after you had received his written report, that Jennings brought his concerns to my office. Exactly what period of time do you feel should be given to a supervisor to initiate some form of inquiry into as serious a situation as embezzlement?

"If memory serves, when I visited you to establish what indeed you were doing, you appeared ignorant of the problem. You also denied having received a report from Jennings and said you could remember no hint of anything out of the ordinary. Well, lady, if you consider misappropriation of funds as ordinary, we are in bigger trouble than I realized."

"I didn't mean it that way" said Suzanne, in an attempt to defend her actions.

"You assured me you would, and I quote, 'leave no stone unturned in my quest for the truth'. A bit dramatic, I admit, but those were your exact words." Aware of Ms. Carson's flair for the dramatic, no one in the room doubted the accuracy of the quotation.

"I, too, gave you sufficient time to prove you could handle an assignment, which fell within the bounds of your authority. But, as Jennings had before me, I became frustrated with your delay tactics. So, I went to your mother. It was only after she learned of the difficulty that the matter was resolved. Could you please explain to me how, knowing we are enlightened as to your conduct throughout this fiasco, you can now sit there and take credit for the successful outcome, though apparently temporary, of the matter?" Timothy was one of those rare individuals who can remain articulate in the midst of their fury.

"I think we would all like to hear your answer to that one," added Melissa. "Not to mention why you felt justified in ignoring such a potentially hazardous threat. Did you not realize the irreparable damage which may have resulted, by allowing such a matter to continue? I find it impossible to believe that anyone could be that irresponsible." Melissa was feeling the contagious effects of Timothy's righteous indignation.

"Just wait a minute! I do not have to sit here and be insulted. I was extremely busy when Simon brought the matter to my attention, overwhelmed by more pressing issues which could not be postponed." Suzanne did not feel it prudent to mention that the most pressing decision occupying her mind, at the time in question, was where she could obtain a suitable gown for the posh affair she was invited to attend that evening, at the Bedford estate. She also felt it inadvisable to admit that she knew who had been falsifying the orders. To admit that would invite suspicion on the part of the others that she had participated in the theft. No, it was best to go along with their belief that the problem had been successfully rectified by her mother. "When Mr. Hudson mentioned Jennings' report, I said that was the first I had heard of it. I had forgotten about Simon's visit."

"Did you not read the report when it appeared on your desk?" asked Melissa.

"No. I just got through telling you, I was too busy. When things slackened off, I forgot about the report. Don't you ever forget anything?" Suzanne directed her accusation toward Mel, hoping that by doing so, she could divert the attack away from herself. Ms. Carson usually enjoyed being the center of attention. Contrarily, on this occasion, she would have preferred to be on the outside, looking in.

"We all have a tendency to forget things," admitted Melissa. "Although, rarely, have I known anyone to forget something of such importance. If you felt there was a chance of your overlooking the report, it would have been beneficial to leave a note to yourself as a reminder. For that matter, if you were under too much pressure or too overworked to handle the problem expediently, you should have referred Jennings to Mr. Hudson." Melissa was not gullible enough to believe her cousin was ever overworked, at least not in the normal sense of the word. Obviously her definition did not coincide with Suzanne's.

"If I asked Mr. Hudson to handle the problem, explaining I was too busy to do so, he would have gone to Mother, complaining about my inability to do my job. I did not need her getting on my case, one more time, about my lack of responsibility. She was constantly telling me I was unable to put things in proper perspective.

"To my way of thinking, people around here worry too much. This is a prime example of what I mean. Why are you all getting so bent out of shape over a small error in ordering? An error which has already been rectified." Suzanne decided that, if the innocent, overworked excuse was unacceptable (which by the reactions of her interrogators, appeared to be the case), perhaps the preferable approach to employ would be one of trying to minimize the problem.

"Suzanne, you have got to be kidding?" Donald had been

listening intently to the verbal bantering between his sister and the others, unable to believe what he was hearing.

"What do you mean?" responded Suzanne, hoping Donald had not joined forces against her. Her hopes were dashed by his next comment.

"Even you cannot be that stupid! We are discussing a plot which, as I understand it, divested this company of several thousands of dollars." Donald was aghast at her failure to grasp the significance of the situation.

"But, it was settled. The danger is over. Besides, I think you are all exaggerating the amount the company lost. An extra order or two could hardly be worth that much."

"Ms. Sommers, if I may speak?" Jennings politely began and, with an affirmative nod from Melissa, continued. "Ms. Carson, I advised you at the time that my concern was due to the number of extra orders. There had been three incidents, within a month span. Probably more. That is cause for concern. I would not have been alarmed over one extra order."

"Okay, so there were several orders." Suzanne's tone denoted frustration. "I still fail to understand why you are dredging up something that happened months ago and was already taken care of."

The woman was beginning to tire of the abuse she was receiving. All for the sake of her lover. Well, it was too late to turn back now.

In a way, the others were right. If she had taken the time to read Jennings' report, she may have been able to gain control of the situation sooner. She had been derelict in her duties, in that regard.

"You don't, by any chance, have knowledge of whom was found accountable?" Timothy directed his query toward both Carsons.

"Timothy," answered Donald, "I can honestly say I knew nothing of this trouble, before you spoke with Suzanne and myself. Suzanne had not advised me of Jennings' report, nor told me of his visit to her office. When you came to us with the problem, I was in the midst of some rather complicated transactions. Suzanne assured me she could look into the matter without my assistance. Had I not been under the gun to complete the business I was handling, I would have pursued the issue myself. In the future, I will refrain from leaving business of any significance, in the hands of my sister."

A sharp rap on the door to the conference room signified the arrival of the accounting staff. Following a brief introduction to the topic being discussed, Melissa addressed the assembly. "Does anyone here know what information Mrs. Carson's investigation disclosed? Specifically, if she learned who was responsible?"

The response to her question was general nods of denial by members of the audience. One young girl raised her hand.

"Yes," acknowledged Melissa, recognizing the employee as the lady Timothy had introduced to her as Meredith Walker, a new addition to the accounting department within the past year. She was described as a pleasant girl who was proving to be a dedicated and competent accountant.

A shy individual, Meredith spoke only when she felt what she had to say was important. "Mrs. Carson came into the office one day asking questions about the people I worked with. She was very nice, apologizing for taking me from my duties. I answered her questions as best I could. They were mostly in reference to whom worked late on certain nights. Who covered the office during lunch breaks? And were there occasions when any of the staff were left in the office alone for an extended period of time? I told her that protocol dictated there were to be no less than two accountants present in the accounting department, at all times. I sensed she already knew that and was perhaps merely testing me. I explained that the other accountant working with me at the time she dropped in had just stepped out to the washroom. In fact, he returned before she finished speaking with me.

"She also asked if I knew any of the stock room employees. I told her I was unacquainted with the personnel employed in that department, aside from exchanging casual greetings in the cafeteria, or when arriving and departing from work. She thanked me for my help, spoke briefly with my co-worker and left."

"Thanks, Meredith," Timothy appreciated the girl speaking out, conscious of her tendency to remain silent, especially in meetings. "I guess we have no way of finding out what Judith's inquiry revealed, as she is not here to fill us in. Since the activities ceased, for a period of time, I feel it is safe to assume she was instrumental in that outcome."

"You don't think this business had anything to do with her death, do you?" demanded Suzanne. Mel was not the only one to notice her cousin's sudden pallor.

"It is doubtful that someone stealing the money from the agency would have access to the mansion. I think we can omit our thief from the list of suspects, if anyone had considered that probability." Donald felt the two events, if connected, were loosely hinged.

"For the moment, we will treat the events independently," said Timothy. "I agree with Donald. It is highly unlikely that the same person is responsible for both crimes. Not, that is, unless he had an accomplice at the estate. If we are given any reason to suspect there could be a connection, we will inform the police immediately.

"For now, we have a more pressing problem. Recently, a matter has been brought to my attention. A case of double-billing to one of our clients. Although, I am doubtful that the matter is limited to one company, I have only been informed of one incident.

"The primary bill was paid, as per procedure. Promptly and in full. Subsequently, another bill was sent requesting further monies, under the guise of unexpected last minute increased production costs. The sum received in the second payment was not deposited in the agency account and we have no record of that bill ever being sent."

"Do we have a copy of the second bill. If so, is it authentic?" asked Donald.

"Actually, we have obtained the original copy. The bill was printed on agency stationary, with our stamp affixed to it.

The bill displays Mr. Jennings' signature, a signature he adamantly denies signing. We plan to take the incriminating document to a handwriting expert to verify the authenticity of the signature, though I am inclined to believe Simon."

"If it is a forgery, how do you propose we find out who wrote it?" Suzanne asked, wishing to redeem herself, by showing genuine interest in the situation. Surely her friend was not mixed up in this scheme, so soon after the other incident.

"Since all our bill forms are kept in the accounting department, we must assume a member of that staff is somehow involved." Before Timothy had an opportunity to conclude his phrase, gasps were emitted from the employees included in this group. Shocked expressions accompanied the verbal outcry. "Just a second. Let me finish. The extra bill could only be sent from the accounting department. Therefore, it would have to be someone who works there or another employee who gained illegal entry into that section.

"I wish to make it clear that all staff with keys to that area will be interviewed. We have considered the likelihood that the key was obtained without the owner's knowledge. You may have misplaced it, or had it stolen. Our thief could have had it copied. If any of you remember losing your key and having it returned to you, or retrieving it from the lost and found department, please advise us of the circumstances behind the temporary loss.

"If you noticed someone from a different department, hanging around your section, especially if you thought their presence suspicious or, in any way, inappropriate, we want to be informed. Even if it seemed insignificant, at the time. It may help us.

"Please do not allow fear of reprisal to deter you from approaching us. As you can understand, it is urgent we gain control of this situation as soon as possible. We can do this more readily if we all work together."

Melissa addressed the group. "We should exercise all options and check out any avenue open to us. I will remind you, we do not want to endanger any employee. Therefore, it would be best to bring any ideas you may have to us, as opposed to pursuing your suspicions alone. We have no way of knowing what type of person we are dealing with, or what they will do, if cornered.

"If no one has anything more to offer, we should adjourn. As Timothy suggested, it is unlikely this is restricted to one client company. It is important we keep our eyes and ears open for any irregularities. By doing so, we may be able to avert the next occurrence. Thank you and good day."

With the conclusion of the conference, the members dispersed to their delegated duties. Most of them were deep in thought, trying to recall even the smallest particle of information, in hopes it could shed some light on the predicament facing the agency. As convinced as Timothy and Melissa were of Simon's innocence, they deeply resented the obvious frame-up of a man they truly loved and admired.

14

Following the meeting, Mr. Hudson's first stop was the mail room. Here he reviewed a copy of the schedule for the day mentioned on the bogus supply requisition. From the schedule he learned the information he needed. The messenger delivering to the fifth floor on the day in question was Mark Dunn. Ironically, the man was no longer employed at Carson Agency.

With further scrutiny he learned that the man had been relieved of service two days after Timothy had spoken with Judith in regard to the embezzlement threat. This new data implied a possible connection between Mr. Dunn and the embezzlers. If so, Mrs. Carson must have learned of it and fired him.

In order to prove his theory, Timothy decided to take steps

to clarify if, indeed, it was Judith's decision to order Dunn's release. Toward that end, he left a message with the employee currently manning the phones at the messenger station advising Jeffrey Marsh, the mail room supervisor, to meet with him, when the latter finished his lunch break.

When he returned to his office, Timothy notified Melissa of his findings. She found the facts very interesting, agreeing that it was unreasonable to put the young man's dismissal down as merely coincidental, considering how soon it occurred after Timothy's talk with Judith. Timothy advised her of his expected chat with Mr. Marsh, inviting her to attend.

Melissa's arrival at Timothy's office preceded the appearance of the mail room supervisor by a mere five minutes, preventing further discussion.

"Thank you for coming so promptly, Jeffrey," Tim began. "A matter has come to my attention and I wish to discuss it with you."

"Yes, sir," responded Mr. Marsh.

"Jeffrey, there was a young man working for you a few months back. I have recently learned he was let go. Do you remember the reason for Mark Dunn's dismissal and who authorized his release?"

"Well, sir, I was the person who advised him he was fired, but it was through no complaint of mine that he was let go. Actually, he was one of my best workers. Always on time, cheerful, got along well with everyone and did his job superbly."

"I don't understand," remarked Timothy. "If he was so good at his job, why was he fired?"

"Really, sir, I have not the vaguest idea. It was a managerial decision, overriding my authority. I was simply instructed to inform him that his services were no longer required. He was to pack up his belongings and leave before close of business hours that day. I was given explicit orders to guarantee he did not return, advising him we would mail his severance pay."

"So it was Judith who found sufficient basis for his

dismissal." Timothy was proud of his deductive reasoning. If Mrs. Carson had ordered the action, that would support his theory that the young man was participating in the embezzlement at the time of his release.

"No, sir, it wasn't Mrs. Carson. It was her daughter who called me."

Timothy was surprised by this bit of news. "Did Ms. Carson provide any indication of dissatisfaction with Mr. Dunn's employment record?"

"No, and when I questioned her as to what explanation I should give him, warranting his termination of employment, she became hostile, telling me I had no business questioning her direction. I was merely to follow her orders."

"Well, that sure sounds like Suzanne," pointed out Melissa, unnecessarily. "How did Mr. Dunn react to news of his discharge?"

"He was, understandably, upset. Wanting to know why he was being released and by whom the decision had been made. I told him I was not free to divulge that information. If he wanted further clarification, I advised him to contact Ms. Carson. He saw little point in doing so, stating his belief that she would only make excuses anyway. Considering her general attitude toward employees, he was probably right. Little would be accomplished by voicing a complaint. He just packed up his things and left. Pausing only long enough to ask me for a reference, which I assured him I would willingly supply."

"Why was I not apprised of these developments at the time?" asked Timothy.

"I offered to notify you but Ms. Carson said, as it was her decision, it was her responsibility to inform you. I was unaware she had not done so."

"Thank you, Jeffrey, that will be all. If we have any more questions we will contact you, or if you think of anything you wish to add, please get in touch with me."

"I can only think of one thing, sir."

"Yes?"

"Just my opinion of her action, sir. It wasn't fair. Ms.

Carson had no right to order me to fire that young man without any explanation as to why. He was a good worker. It just wasn't fair."

Rarely had Timothy seen the man display such emotion. It was clear he was disturbed by Suzanne's high handed approach and did not feel her action was justified. Mr. Marsh was not the type of employee who normally questioned or resented those in authority. If he were telling the truth, and Timothy had no reason to believe otherwise, his reaction to Suzanne's conduct was warranted. "I can understand your confusion and anger. I would feel the same way. Believe me, Jeffrey, I will have a little chat with Ms. Carson."

"It is not my place to question the decision of my superiors and it is something I rarely do. But wrong is wrong, sir. I don't care if she was the owner's daughter, what she did was wrong!" With this, Jeffrey departed.

"He certainly is upset with Suzanne," said Mel. "Apparently with good reason."

"He is not the only one. She does not have the authority to fire an employee without clearing it with me, or, at that time, with her mother. Somehow, I doubt Judith would have given her approval to such a decision. Not without sufficient cause. If there were adequate grounds for Dunn's termination, I want to know what they were. And why she failed to inform me of her decision to release him. If she knew her decision was justified there would have been no reason to avoid telling me."

Timothy placed the call demanding, not requesting, Suzanne's presence in his office without delay. As expected, the reception to his demand was a cool one.

"Is that really necessary?" she asked.

"Yes, I'm afraid it is," was the man's response.

"Fine. I will be there shortly." Timothy heard the phone slam in his ear. An immature reaction, but, typically Suzanne.

Surprisingly enough, Suzanne arrived promptly. As usual, she immediately assumed an offensive approach. "Isn't this a bit repetitive? I thought we had discussed everything. What am I being blamed for now?"

"Don't worry, Suzanne, we intend to make that perfectly clear," said Timothy. "I have two questions for you. Number one, what was your rationale for dismissing Mark Dunn? Secondly, why did you neglect advising me of your decision to do so?"

"In answer to your first question, he was released for insubordination. In response to your second, it merely slipped my mind. The day he was dismissed, I intended on informing you of my decision, but you were not in your office."

"Was your mother aware of your action?"

"Of course. She totally agreed with his release, under the circumstances." As Judith was not available to refute the lie, Suzanne knew she was safe.

"Really, and what exactly were those circumstances you make reference to?"

"His behavior was disrespectful toward someone in my position."

"Could you be a bit more specific? What, exactly, did he do that was so out of line?"

"He continually made suggestive comments, accompanied by lewd glances, when he delivered mail to my office. I was tired of it."

"Why would Mr. Dunn have any contact with you when he delivered mail to your office? Isn't that something your secretary would normally take care of?" asked Melissa.

Suzanne hesitated, momentarily, before answering. "There were times when she had stepped out of the office. Rather than leave it on her desk, he brought it to me directly. His excuse was that he wanted to make sure I received it."

"We understand you felt it unnecessary to offer an explanation to Mr. Dunn or, for that matter his immediate supervisor, as to the reason for his release. Ms. Carson, if you are in the habit of instructing others to do your dirty work, don't you think you could at least tell them why you feel the action is necessary?" Timothy was frustrated with the antics of this self-serving female.

"I don't know what you are talking about!"

"In speaking with Mr. Marsh he informed us you told him, over the telephone, to relieve Mr. Dunn of his position with this company. You refused to supply Mr. Marsh, despite his request for one, a reasonable explanation for that directive. Is that not so?"

"Mr. Hudson, I do not have to defend my decisions to employees under my charge. I gave him an order and I expected him to carry it. Without question, and without delay. If I had felt an explanation was necessary, he would have received one. His approval was not required."

"I'm surprised you can find justification for postponing your own duties, when you cannot tolerate similar behavior in others."

"Oh, God. Are you going to bring up the business with those stock orders again? We have already beat that subject to death."

"Yes we have, and I do not intend on discussing it further. For now."

"Thank God." Suzanne was obviously relieved.

"Ms. Carson, while it is true you have no obligation to explain your decisions to those employees under your supervision, in an attempt to maintain good company relations, it is beneficial to appear approachable.

"I take it you are unfamiliar with labor laws which state that no employee can be relieved of duty without just cause. An employer who disregards this law can be brought up, quite successfully I might add, on charges by said employee. Perhaps you would have been wise to consider this probability, prior to making such a rash decision."

"Oh, now I get it. Mark Dunn is suing us for unjustified dismissal. So what, we have enough money. Pay him off and be done with it."

"You are awfully free-spending with company funds, Suzanne. Although he has every right to do so I have not heard of any suit by Mr. Dunn. You can count yourself fortunate on that score.

"As usual, I fail to understand your thinking. We are

talking, not only of a man's reputation. This accusation could have affected his career as well. With the lack of job opportunities available, due to the recession, he may have run into difficulty procuring work elsewhere. If a prospective employer were to look into the cause for Mr. Dunn's dismissal, he would hesitate before hiring someone previously released for charges of insubordination."

"Really, Mr. Hudson, that is hardly my concern. If he had wanted to continue working here, he should have behaved in a more appropriate and professional manner.

"If my sources are as reliable as I believe them to be, this conversation is redundant. I have been told the man has found suitable employment elsewhere. That being the case, his career has obviously not been as adversely affected as you surmised it would."

"Ms. Carson, the fact that Mr. Dunn was able to procure gainful employment after his dismissal is solely due to Mr. Marsh's intervention. Had it not been for him, Mark's career would have been in the dumpster."

"As I said, I do not see that as being my problem."

"No, I didn't think you would. But I thought it was worth a try. Appealing to your sense of fair play and compassion, that is. In the off chance a similar situation arises in future, you may wish to consider the possible ramifications of such a response before you abruptly dismiss someone else."

"I would hope that future employees will know the proper way to conduct themselves, in the presence of people superior to them."

"You were Mr. Dunn's supervisor, Ms. Carson. That does not imply, in any way, that you were superior to him. Merely more fortunate."

Melissa, at this juncture, assumed control of the interrogation. "Suzanne," she began, "I am having a bit of trouble comprehending how you could have such problems with a man you had limited contact with. The same man who elicited such glowing recommendations from his immediate supervisor. Mr. Marsh described Mark as an excellent worker, cheerful and pleasant to all. Why would he single you out to harass?"

"I don't know. He probably had difficulty accepting women in positions of authority. It threatens some men to have to answer to a female."

Melissa, though aware of such cases occurring, was disturbed by a nagging feeling there was an ingredient missing in Suzanne's claim. The description she gave of Mark's attitude toward her did not correspond with the overall impression she had been given of the young man. Knowing Suzanne's ego, where the opposite sex was concerned, Mel surmised Suzanne would be more upset if the man did not afford her the attention she felt she deserved. It was uncharacteristic for her to respond to flirtatious overtures by firing the man who made them.

"Suzanne, did anything in particular happen the day you ordered Mr. Dunn's release? Had he done something specific to force your hand?" inquired Melissa.

"Why do you ask?" Not wishing to dig a deeper hole for herself, Suzanne felt it wise to establish what inspired Melissa's question, before she offered a reply.

"Mr. Marsh states you were very insistent that the man leave the premises before the end of the work day and not to return. To insure he would have no reason to do so, you instructed his supervisor to arrange to mail him what pay he was due. His comments led us to believe that possibly an event had transpired earlier that day. An event which left you no option but to fire him."

"No. It was more a culmination of various inappropriate gestures and comments, none of which were outstanding alone but, collectively, could not be tolerated. That day was no exception. I had previously warned him that he would be released if his attitude did not improve. It didn't, so I advised Mr. Marsh to let him go."

"So, you did warn him he was to be fired," commented Mel.

"Yes, on more than one occasion."

"Can you explain to us why, if you advised him of the action you were planning, he was so astonished when Mr.

Marsh spoke with him?" Melissa was bemused by the conflicting reports. With all that had taken place since her involvement in agency affairs, Melissa was not inclined to
accept Suzanne's recollection of anything.

"I suppose he thought I would not go through with it. Well,
he was wrong." Suzanne's tone lacked its normal conviction,
causing Mel to wonder if the woman was regretting her
participation in Mark's discharge.

"Fine, Suzanne, that will be all," said Melissa, indicating
the meeting was over.

After the woman's departure, Melissa voiced her doubts
over what element of truth could be found in Suzanne's
statement. "Her answers were too generalized. If Mr. Dunn
had behaved so abominably, you'd think she could remember
specific comments he made. I know if I fired someone over
inappropriate behavior, I would be able to provide more
details than she has given us, as to why."

"You'd probably have everything written down and dated,"
laughed Timothy.

"Damn right," confirmed Mel.

"The only way we will know what actually went on
between those two is to meet with our former messenger and
get his version of the facts. There is one thing bothering me,
though."

"What is that?"

"If Mark felt his firing was undeserved, why did he leave
without protest?"

"He's the only one who can answer that question," stated
Melissa. "Maybe he realized it was her word against his. She
was the owner's daughter. He was just an employee. Who do
you think people would believe?"

"You've got a point. Though anyone who knew Suzanne
would probably listen to him."

"Yes. That is true. But, even if he won his case, she could
make his life miserable. Hardly seems worth the effort."

If the amateur sleuths had been privy to the conversation
being conducted, at that moment, between Suzanne and her

male acquaintance, they would have obtained some vital information.

"We have a big problem," Suzanne announced dramatically, upon arriving at the motel.

"Really, and what might that be?" asked the man, impatiently. Suzanne had kept him waiting over an hour. His mood was far from pleasant when she finally showed up. He had considered leaving but thought better of it. For now, he wanted to keep her on the string.

"They are asking questions. Questions I can't answer, to do with Mark Dunn's dismissal. I told you, at the time, I needed more ammunition to pull it off, without creating suspicion. A few suggestive comments, though worthy of reprimand, hardly qualify as reason for firing someone.

"What if they talk to him? They will discover that I hardly knew the man. I only spoke to him a couple of times. Besides, it hardly seems right to accuse a man of conduct he did not display. The only thing he ever said to me when he delivered my mail was a polite 'Good day, ma'am'. I don't think anyone is going to be convinced that he meant it as a sexual overture. What have I allowed you to get me into?

"And, another thing." Suzanne was on a roll. Not stopping long enough for her companion to respond. "Why didn't you tell me he was so damn popular? It's like making an accusation against a local hero. He has the reputation of a bloody saint."

"I thought you said no one would question your decision to let him go." The man interjected, while he had a chance.

"Normally, they wouldn't. But, Melissa is so intent on proving herself, she is looking into everything that is out of the ordinary. She found out about the business with those orders you falsified and she is on a mission to solve the puzzle. God, I wish I had never let you talk me into firing him."

"You know we had no choice. There was no other way to keep what we are doing a secret. He was getting too close to finding out our arrangement. It would have been too dangerous, allowing him to stay on and risk exposure. Surely you can see that."

"But if those two meddlers talk to him, our secret will be out anyway. And, with it, the identity of the embezzler."

"Don't worry about Mark. I will take care of him. You just concentrate on holding yourself together. It would never do for the staff to find out that the exalted Ms. Carson has been sleeping with someone beneath her. Pardon the pun."

Suzanne missed the veiled threat in the man's comment. She was more troubled by what he meant by taking care of Mark. To date, she could honestly say she had never been a party to anything remotely considered violent. Nor was she about to.

Sure, she had taken up with an employee (a type of relationship she had been warned was seldom wise and sometimes detrimental to any kind of productive professional association). A union, she preferred, remain private. Mostly because she could not handle the embarrassment if anyone found out. She knew this was her own doing, voicing her negative opinions of those not of her social background.

It was true, she had covered up her knowledge of his efforts to steal money from the company. But, when she found out what he had done, she warned him to stop. And he had. Although, from the news recently received from Timothy and Melissa, it appeared he may have resumed his activities in that regard.

Well, Mother was gone now. Only the fear of her finding out about Suzanne's association with the embezzler forced Judith's daughter to speak with her lover about the previous episode.

She now debated asking him about the recent events at the agency. But, why should she? If she left well enough alone, Melissa would have to look after the matter. Maybe that is just what her meddlesome cousin needed, to convince her to relinquish ownership.

No, she would leave things as they were. It served Mel right. Lording her new position over Suzanne. Why should she do anything to help Melissa? Anyway, if she told Mel of her suspicions, her cousin was sure to believe Suzanne had helped the man.

Besides, her lover possessed a violent temper. Were he to find out that she had turned him in, Suzanne would be on the receiving end of that temper. Not a pleasant prospect.

She admitted she had been a bit, well perhaps more than a bit, short-sighted in fulfilling her lover's request for Mark Dunn's removal from the agency. Had she known the real reason behind the request, she would have denied it. Or, at least, she could tell herself that now.

Otherwise, she could see no area where her judgment was erroneous. Realistically, she had created for herself some potentially hazardous situations, through her dubious choices and her silence. But, so far, she was unscathed. With any luck, her good fortune would continue. The slightest indication of further trouble however, would necessitate extricating herself from the relationship and denying any association with the man, or his activities. To make her story believable she would have to be better prepared than she was for the meeting today. A performance which was laughable, at best.

Meanwhile, the two people who were causing Ms. Carson all the grief were planning, though unconsciously, to add to her woes. They had arranged a meeting with Mark Dunn to discuss the circumstances surrounding his involuntary departure from the agency. The young man appeared eager to have his say.

Suzanne's friend had other plans. Ms. Carson and Mark Dunn were liabilities. Liabilities which must be dealt with. He had figured out a way to "kill two birds with one stone," so to speak. Dispose of both of his problems with one act.

God, he was smart. Very smart. How else could he think up such brilliant schemes. If only more people would realize how clever he truly was. They would. That he would see to personally.

15

The second complaint of double billing was not long in being reported. Immediately after his conversation with Mark Dunn, Timothy's secretary announced an incoming call from one Elroy Jackson, owner of a chain of hardware stores. Mr. Jackson's case was similar, in all aspects but one, to that of Seymour Allen, including the presence of Simon Jennings' signature on the accompanying letter of explanation. The only difference: the man was reporting the second bill prior to remitting payment and was refusing to pay the additional sum requested.

It was apparent, from his tone, that Mr. Jackson was not prepared to be as easily appeased as their other client had been. He reminded the assistant manager of the sizable advertising account he held with the agency. "Never, in all my years of dealing with your company, have I been exposed to such an outrage. In the event of necessary price hikes in the past, I was notified, prior to the completion of the current ad campaign. And, I might add, was supplied with a complete breakdown as to the outlay of funds, not merely a vague reference to increased production costs. To be informed of this unforeseen, additional charge in the present fashion is unprofessional for an agency of your status and totally unacceptable. Young man, I want an explanation and I want it now!" The volume of the man's oral outburst increased steadily with each syllable pronounced.

Timothy thanked the man for drawing the problem to his attention. He then proceeded to explain their predicament. Unfortunately, the honest approach which had been so effective in dealing with Mr. Allen, was lost on this client. Mr. Jackson was beyond the point of reason.

"The difficulties you are experiencing are not my concern. I advise you to get the situation under control and speedily. If you do not succeed in doing so the reputation of Carson Agency is certain to be adversely affected by these developments. It is one thing to have internal difficulties, quite another to have those difficulties interfere with client relations. Should these incidents become common knowledge you are sure to find yourself in a major quagmire.

"I will make you one promise. That I do, only out of respect for Mrs. Carson. One hell of a woman, by the way, and one who always treated me fairly. To be honest, I doubt I would ever have gotten anywhere in this business, if not for her and Howard.

"I promise, for now, I will refrain from spreading the news of this incident to my colleagues. Don't get me wrong by assuming my fondness for your former employer will influence my decision, should this feeble attempt to milk my company of extra funds be repeated. If that should happen, I will be forced to take my advertising business elsewhere.

"More importantly, at that time, I will feel obligated to

advise my associates, who hold accounts with your agency, to do the same. As you, no doubt, are aware, I wield a fair bit of power and influence in the business community. Were I to offer my advertising account to one of your competitors, others would do the same, even without my personal recommendation. Not to mention the sizable annual income your company would forfeit with the loss of such a lucrative account. Have I made myself clear?"

"Perfectly," said Timothy, fully aware of the impact such an event could have on the agency.

"He was right you know," Timothy directed this comment to Melissa, after outlining what Mr. Jackson had said. "If this continues much longer, it will place us in a sticky situation with many of our clients. Should word of this get out, it will be almost impossible to convince anyone that they would be best served remaining with us. It takes a lot longer to build up a reputation, than it does to tear it down. That is true, as much in business, as it is in one's personal life."

"We must make every effort to insure that doesn't happen," stated Melissa, forcefully. "Judith and Howard spent too many years building this agency up to where it is, to have it wrecked in a fraction of that time. It is vital that we find the solution and nip this thing in the bud, before the damage becomes irreparable.

"We have been fortunate so far. Our luck will not continue much longer. We must use this period of grace to our advantage."

"Agreed. Let's hope our meeting with Mr. Dunn provides some important insight into the matter. If we are no further ahead, after speaking with him, we may wish to review our options."

"What options?" asked Mel.

"Well, we could consider dispatching a memo to each of our clients, advising them of the situation we are presently facing. By doing so we may be able to prevent a repeat performance."

"Do you think we should wait any longer, before releasing such a memo?"

"I think it best to hold out for a bit. We do not want to alarm clients unnecessarily. If the embezzlers know of our inquiry, they may cease their activity, until they find out if we are making any headway. If so, the two cases reported may be all there are. Those men have promised not to leak out the information and they are men of their word.

"People in business tend to become nervous easily. If they learn we are in the midst of an embezzlement threat, they may become concerned that our attentions are being drawn elsewhere. Their advertising business may be taken to our competitors, if they fear this matter will detract from the quality of our work."

"I see what you mean."

"Surely, between the interview with Mark and our consultation with the handwriting expert, we will be further ahead than we are now."

"I certainly hope so," remarked Melissa, her statement receiving a nod of confirmation from Timothy.

They arrived at Mark's apartment at the appointed hour. Simon Jennings, who knew the young man, had agreed to accompany them. The trio thought this wise, feeling Mark would be less threatened by someone familiar.

After waiting thirty minutes, with no sign of the young man, Simon appeared worried, "This is not like Mark. He was always very punctual when he worked with us. If anything, he tended to be early. Perhaps we should check with the building superintendent to find out if he has seen him."

"Why don't you do that, Simon?" suggested Timothy. "In the meanwhile, I will phone his office. Perhaps he was delayed."

The man answering Tim's call was a friend of Mark's. "Mark left about two hours ago," he said. "He told me about the meeting and seemed in a hurry to get home so as not to be late. He didn't say he had any stops to make on the way. Even if he had, I think he would have postponed them."

Thanking the man, Timothy returned to the others with what he had learned. Upon his return, Simon presented a key to Mark's apartment. One he had obtained from the super. The man had relinquished the key only after verifying Simon's identity and inquiring as to the reason for his visit. The superintendent gave the visitors more cause for concern over Mark's well-being when he told them he had seen the young man return to his apartment an hour before Simon and the others arrived.

Prior to inserting the key in the lock, Timothy firmly rapped on the door, repeating the action he had done when they initially arrived. As noted previously, there was no answer to his knock. As he unlocked the door, he warned Melissa to stay behind the two men until they surveyed the apartment, verifying if it was safe to enter.

The sight that greeted their entry was far from pleasant. A young man lying prone on the living room carpet, with a sizable dent in the back of his skull. It was evident, even before Mel checked for a pulse, that none would be detected. Mark Dunn was dead and not by his own hand. The tire iron lying beside the body attested to that.

The three, simultaneously, came to the conclusion, accurate or not, that his murder was directly related to their scheduled meeting. With this conjecture, came the logical supposition that Suzanne Carson, being the only person aware of their investigation into Mark's dismissal from the agency, must be involved in his murder. Fearing he would reveal facts harmful to her best interests, Suzanne must have convinced herself that his permanent removal was in order. The most troubling realization in all of this was that, by displaying a desire to learn more about the man's release they had, inadvertently, placed him in mortal danger.

Timothy notified the building manager of their findings. Making use of his phone, the police were also informed. Once again, Officer Rawlins was the detective dispatched to the scene of the crime. "You do tend to get around, don't you," he remarked, recognizing Melissa. "May I ask what your association was with the victim?"

The female of the group illuminated the purpose for their visit, omitting any reference to her cousin, or to the fact that

Suzanne was instrumental in Mark's termination of employment. "We learned he left the agency a short time ago and wanted to check into his reasons for doing so."

"I see. So, you have no idea who would be interested in seeing him dead."

"Afraid not, Officer." Mel chose to overlook the accusatory glances she was receiving from her companions, hoping that Detective Rawlins did the same. Mel felt it could be advantageous to keep Suzanne's participation in Mark's departure out of the facts revealed. She hoped, by facing her cousin with their allegations, the woman would, unwittingly, mention something incriminating. Mel deduced the only way to penetrate the coat of armor Suzanne encased herself in was through the element of surprise.

Were Rawlins to learn of her connection with the deceased, he may interpret it as a motive for murder. If arrested, Suzanne was sure to clam up and they would get nothing out of her. They had to try to find out what she was hiding through some ingenuity and, to a degree, fear tactics. Melissa was uncomfortable employing the latter, but time did not permit subtleties.

Simon, being the one who knew Mark personally, provided what details he could about the young man, reminding the officer that he had not seen Mark for some time and knew little of his acquaintances and personal habits. His primary exposure to the man had been by way of his employment. An employment that ended rather abruptly. Following Melissa's lead, although he did not approve of withholding information from the authorities, Simon refrained from expounding on the man's departure from the agency and the fact his exodus was not a voluntary one.

"Well, folks," Rawlins announced, "if that is all you can tell me, and I sincerely hope it is, you are free to go. I will be making an official visit to your offices tomorrow, to interview those employees who knew the deceased."

"Fine, Detective," said Timothy, "I will instruct everyone to offer their full cooperation."

Leaving the police to their duties, the trio departed.

"This is more than mere coincidence," proclaimed Mel. "First, we learn the identity of the person who delivered the bogus stock order. Then we check into it, only to discover the man has been relieved of service, under controversial circumstances. And now, to top things off, when we arrange to meet with this individual, he winds up dead. Murdered. There is no possible way these events are not connected.

"I think it is time to visit the mansion. I'm going to find out what it is Suzanne is hiding, supposing I have to shake it out of her. God, a man is dead."

"That reminds me," remarked the younger of her allies, "Why didn't you tell Rawlins that Mark's release was Suzanne's doing? Instead, you made it sound as though the man left voluntarily. You may be placing yourself and the rest of us in an awkward position, should the distinguished gentleman discover your deception."

"He will find that out tomorrow. Right now, I want to use that little tidbit as ammunition to attack Suzanne's psyche. Maybe we can convince her she is in imminent danger of going to prison, should the police learn of the part she played in this whole affair. Especially, if her action was as shady and unwarranted as we have reason to suspect. She may open up to us. Tell us what she knows.

"I don't think she would kill the man herself, but I would not put it past her to go along with the action. First and foremost, that lady is looking out for herself. If she thought Mark posed a threat to her, she would do what she felt she had to do to remove that threat.

"I also get the distinct impression that, whatever is going on, she is not in it alone. I'm not even convinced she is the ringleader, although I find it difficult envisioning her allowing someone else to be in charge. Despite her bravado, she was obviously uncomfortable with the decision to fire Mr. Dunn. Possibly realizing she had no legitimate basis for the action.

"What it boils down to is this, Suzanne Carson has a secret. And, the quickest way to discover what that secret is, is for her to tell us."

16

The drive to the estate was alive with animated conversation. There is nothing like a good mystery to liven up a discussion. Melissa, however, preferred her intrigue in the form of a novel. Where the events did not affect real people. The situation surrounding Mark Dunn was a prime example of how crime touches the innocent. A young man, who did his appointed task to the best of his ability, caught up in circumstances not of his choosing and beyond his control. Circumstances which resulted in his murder. This was not right and if Suzanne was, either directly or indirectly, involved with his death, she must be held accountable for that participation.

Carmelita answered the doorbell's ring and bid them entrance. After confirming that Suzanne and Donald were at home, the maid left the room to announce the visitors. She returned promptly and directed them to the study where the Carsons were partaking of after dinner drinks.

"Good evening, everyone," greeted Donald, his tone welcoming. Suzanne's look, on the other hand, was hostile. "What brings you here at this hour?" the man continued, ignoring his sister's lack of hospitality.

"Sorry to impose, Donald. But, we must speak with your sister," Timothy announced the purpose for their visit. Apologizing for the lack of advance notice, he explained that, due to the urgency of the subject matter, the discussion could not be postponed.

"It is no imposition. Can I offer anyone a drink?" Donald was playing the role of host superbly, despite the fact that his visitors were uninvited. His jovial demeanor irritated the individual with whom the party wished to speak. Suzanne anxiously awaited word on what brought about the unscheduled visit. Obviously, the group wished to lay the blame for some other catastrophe squarely at her feet. She found herself wondering how she could weasel her way out of another sticky situation.

If only Melissa would go away. She had caused nothing but trouble for Suzanne since taking over the reins of the agency. If she would just leave, things could get back to normal.

Donald gave no sign that he was prepared to exit the room. In view of his sister's conduct of late, combined with the antagonistic tone in Timothy's voice, Donald felt it wise to remain for the entire length of the conversation. It was obvious, by the presentation of the troop, the topic to be discussed was serious and, somehow, it appeared they were under the impression Suzanne played an integral role.

"Donald, you are welcome to stay, unless Suzanne has some objection. In response to your kind offer I think, after what we have been through this evening, we could all use a brandy." Timothy expressed gratitude for the suggestion of liquid fortification. His companions, too, welcomed the offering, their nerves a bit jangled after the experience. Though accustomed to death in a hospital setting, this was Melissa's first exposure to murder.

"Don't you think we talked enough this afternoon?" Suzanne made a vain attempt to thwart further harassment.

"Obviously not, or we would not be here now," retorted Timothy.

Melissa, wishing to avoid having the conversation reduced to a shouting match, interrupted the developing unpleasantness.

"Suzanne," she stated, keeping her voice calm, "we will come straight to the point. Mark Dunn is dead. Murdered. We believe his death is related, in some way, with the discussion we had with you earlier today. Now you can either talk with us, or to the police. It is your choice. Either way, we plan to get results. We know you are hiding something and we intend on finding out what it is." The woman would, eventually, have to speak with the police, whether or not she revealed anything to her interrogators, but Melissa hoped her cousin would fail to come to that realization.

"This is some sort of sick joke," responded the startled female. "You are trying to trick me into telling you what you want to hear, just to get you off my back. Well, it is not going to work. I know nothing about any murder." Though starting her speech with her usual aplomb, Suzanne's self-confidence quickly vanished in an outpouring of tears.

Melissa had succeeded in removing the armor, though realized the effect achieved was a transient one. It was important to seize the moment, before the woman had a chance to compose herself.

Suzanne appeared tired. The fact that she had been the focal point of three uncomfortable conversations, in less than twenty-four hours, was a valid reason for fatigue.

"Are you sure he is dead?" Suzanne managed to blurt out, between sobs.

"We just came from his apartment. We were scheduled to meet him there this evening," said Melissa.

"Did you speak with him?"

"We didn't get the chance. He was dead before we arrived. Someone bludgeoned him with a tire iron."

"You wouldn't know anything about that, would you Ms. Carson?" interjected Timothy.

"I already told you, I know nothing about it. Why are you badgering me like this?"

"Suzanne," said Melissa, "we are not accusing you of killing the man. We are simply asking if you know of anyone who would want him dead. For instance, the person who got you to fire him."

"That was my decision, mine and mine alone and I have already given you my reason for ordering it."

This is a hard nut to crack, thought Melissa. Apparently the superficial coat of armor merely concealed a second layer, equally as difficult to penetrate. Her recuperative powers were amazing. One minute weeping and vulnerable. The next, hard as steel.

Electing to change the subject, Melissa asked, "Did you tell anyone about our meeting with you?"

"No, who would I tell? I wanted to forget all about it."

"Suzanne, be reasonable. You must have told someone."

"Could Mr. Dunn have let it slip to an acquaintance?" suggested Donald, who, up until now, had remained silent. Unaccustomed to seeing his sister in a state of genuine emotional discomfort, the man was instinctively driven to relieve her pain, if such a thing were possible.

Sibling relationships are funny that way. In fact, they are quite possibly the most complex and unpredictable facets of human nature. Brothers and sisters, even those who normally have difficulty being civil to each other, have a bond. A bond which dictates that, when one is in trouble, the other instinctively reaches out to provide relief. The mechanics are similar to the workings of any other basic reflex.

The only explanation for such behavior and, generally, the only one required is that "we are a family and blood is thicker than water." What the latter part of the reasoning has to do with the whole issue is unclear. The fact remains, an intrinsic force governs one's behavior when family is involved, a force which overshadows any other natural phenomenon known to man. A compulsion few understand, though most agree is best accepted at face value. Not wishing to negate its effectiveness, through analysis.

"Actually," Melissa embarrassingly admitted, "we did not consider that angle. Timothy, you mentioned that Mark appeared eager to meet with us. Usually, if someone is enthusiastic about an event, he would tell friends or family."

"Come to think of it," stated Tim, "the gentleman who answered the phone at Mark's work place said he was a friend of Mark's and was aware of our planned meeting. If he told one person, there is a chance he told another. Perhaps one of his former associates at Carson Agency. One possibly connected with the embezzlement scheme. They may have feared he knew more than he did. The only way to prevent exposure was to remove Mark. For good."

"I wish we had something more definite to go on," declared Melissa. "We can invent any number of scenarios, but we have nothing to corroborate any of them. God, we don't even know if we are on the right track.

"Suzanne, I still feel you are keeping something vitally important from us. Maybe you know an individual who is capable of such crimes as embezzlement and murder. You may be afraid to speak out for fear he will do the same to you. If so, you would be wise to reconsider your position. These types of situations have a way of coming back around. You may find yourself caught in the middle, whether you want to be or not. If you tell the police what you know, they can protect you. If you don't, should this person turn on you, you may find yourself alone. Considering what happened to Mark, that might not be the best position to find yourself in.

"For that matter, how do you know this individual does not already consider you a threat to the success of his goal, whatever that may be? A threat that, like Mark Dunn, must be removed."

"There is no point, dear cousin, in trying to scare me. I have no idea what you are referring to. Come to think of it, since everything was running smoothly before you took over the controls, perhaps we should suspect you of being associated with those responsible. You would make a dandy ringleader."

As it was evident nothing more would be accomplished by remaining and discussing the situation in more depth, the trio thanked Donald for the brandies and said their goodnights. The stimulating beverage had restored their equilibriums, countering the effects of what they had viewed at Mark's apartment.

Timothy deposited his passengers at the agency's parking lot, where they had left their vehicles prior to setting out together for the meeting. A meeting which, unfortunately, had never taken place.

"It hardly seems fair," Melissa verbalized feelings of guilt. "Our lives will continue, physically unchanged, despite tonight's events, and a man whom I knew, only by name, is no longer among the living. All because of our curiosity."

"I know what you mean, though we mustn't blame ourselves." Timothy attempted to console the young woman. "Had we known we were endangering Mark, by our wishing to speak with him, we would never have scheduled the meeting, or, at least, suggested a less conspicuous place to meet. We had no reason to believe this type of threat existed. Embezzlers rarely resort to violence.

"Given the same information to go on, we would not change anything. We know that. If, for no other reason, than that our motivation was to get to the truth. Personally, although I grieve the loss of a man's life and the loss for his family, I cannot say I regret doing what we did."

"My, we are analytical this evening, aren't we," stated Melissa, an action that effectively served to lighten the mood.

"We must not think the worst. Something is bound to break soon. I'm sure of it." Simon was doing his part to instill a positive attitude into their thinking.

"A born optimist, aren't you, Simon?" Timothy teased the man, though was glad to hear some encouraging feedback.

"In my experience, that's the only way to be. Pessimism causes people to stagnate. When you stagnate, you lose the urge to try. Personally, I refuse to stop trying, or to allow either of you to."

"I agree with you both," stated Mel. "It is rather pleasant being in your company. Under different circumstances, I might even enjoy it."

As they parted, Timothy reminded his boss of their appointment the following morning with the handwriting expert. They had scheduled the consultation for early morning, thus enabling them to report at the office at a reasonable hour. With the unexpected murder of Mark Dunn, they were thankful for the early consultation, hoping to be present when Detective Rawlins interrogated the agency staff. As the policeman had told them of his plan to check several other sources, prior to visiting Carson Agency, they estimated his arrival as early afternoon. Plenty of time for them to keep their appointment and return, without missing any vital information brought out by the questioning. Information they hoped to be privy to.

17

The next morning gave the promise of an exquisite day. A promise attested to by the weather man, who predicted sun, with a few cloudy intervals. Melissa was glad for the clear forecast as they hoped to make good traveling time. The lady they were to see lived approximately sixty minutes outside of town, a distance requiring an hour to cover: barring unforeseen disruptions, such as slow, or heavy, traffic. An unlikely possibility, considering the time of their departure.

Commencing their journey, as planned, at seven A.M., the couple, not wishing to be detained at a restaurant, stopped for take-out coffee and muffins.

The morning was cool, though pleasantly so. Both travelers were clad appropriately for the temperature. Melissa had selected the addition of a hand knit bulky sweater over her blouse and dress pants. Timothy opted for a sports coat, rather than his normal suit jacket, the former providing the desired extra warmth.

"Coffee sure tastes good on a cool morning," commented Melissa, as she cautiously sipped the hot beverage.

"Coffee tastes good anytime," agreed Timothy, "although it especially hits the spot first thing in the morning. Even more so, if the temperature is on the cool side. It is peculiar how the coffee one brews at home is never as satisfying as what they provide at coffee houses. I've gone so far as to purchase their packaged coffee, taken it home and prepared it following the instructions to the letter, but there is still something missing. Mind you, it is good, just not as good as what they prepare."

"I know. One of the mysteries of life. They must realize, if we could make it as delicious ourselves, our treks to their establishments would be much less frequent. Not very good for business. I believe they cast a magic spell on the coffee they brew to make it particularly stimulating. That way, the customer keeps returning."

"Sounds logical to me," laughed Timothy. "Perhaps I should suggest that angle for their new ad campaign, when it comes up for review."

"That must be a very prestigious account."

"Indeed it is. That is one company I would prefer not get wind of our recent trouble. The general manager is a no-nonsense type of fellow, who has little patience for business disturbances. Let's hope we can solve this dilemma before informing him becomes necessary."

Though not adverse to driving with a fair degree of speed, Timothy refused to sacrifice caution, in its pursuit. In just under the allotted hour, they arrived at their destination.

The person they planned to consult was renown in the district for her expertise in graphology. Though no longer a young woman, she gave no indication of declining competence in her field. Following extensive examination of the signatures and comparison checks with the handwriting samples received from both men involved, Cynthia Newton proclaimed that, despite being excellent forgeries, they were precisely that. And both signatures were, as Timothy and Mel had suspected, by the same hand.

"Well, at least that clears Simon and Mr. Dalton of any blame," remarked Mel, relieved their trust in the two was deserved.

"Can you provide us with any clues as to the type of person responsible for the forgeries?" asked Timothy. The main reason for visiting Mrs. Newton, as opposed to several other experts in the area, was her ability to uncover certain personality traits through reviewing handwriting. Although many people doubted the accuracy of such interpretation, Timothy had learned that much of what Mrs. Newton revealed about individuals in the past, through her handwriting analysis, was later proven to be reliable. Desperate enough to try anything, Timothy was not adverse to giving the woman a shot at it. They risked nothing by calling upon her skills and putting her suggestions into practice. Who knows, it could be helpful. One must keep an open mind about such things.

"There is no doubt the writing is that of a young man. You should focus on someone who displays a good deal of confidence. At times, inappropriately so. He is ambidextrous, though prefers to write left-handed. The precision in the forgery implies someone who is meticulous, almost to the point of being a perfectionist. It is a strong possibility the man you seek has an interest in the arts. My guess would be either painting or sculpture, as he has a definite stroke. That is what gave it away. The fact that the handwriting was forged, I mean." Mrs. Newton pointed out the tendency to exaggerate the sweeping motion ending the signatures.

Thanking the woman for her time, and paying the nominal fee requested, the two made their way back to town, anxious to research their employees, armed with the clues from Mrs. Newton. Despite having been told of the woman's outstanding aptitude in graphology, they were astounded by what she could tell about a person, simply through their handwriting.

During their return trip they discussed how best to put into use the information learned from the expert.

"The two young men working in the accounting department; how much do you know about them?" asked Mel.

"Ted has been with us four years now, Henry six. To my knowledge Jennings has been pleased with their performances. There has been no behavior suggesting noncompliance with company rules and regulations, nor any history of association with unsavory companions."

"Do we know anything about their hobbies or interests. Something which would verify the art angle Mrs. Newton mentioned."

"Possibly. The application form has a section for such details. Judith liked to get to know her employees on a more personal basis, as opposed to simply looking at their resume. By reviewing the form, she learned about their interests outside of the office. She said there were times when she based her final decision on these extraneous facts."

"Is that really fair? Deciding whether or not to hire someone, based on what they do in their private life." Melissa was surprised that her aunt would employ such a method.

"Now don't get me wrong," said Timothy, quickly clarifying his statement. "She did not overplay the importance of an individual's personal life in her assessment of their ability to do the job. However, in the instances where she received several applications from people who were similarly qualified, she often referred to the personal data section to give her more with which to make her choice. It is not obligatory for the applicant to fill in that section of the form, and some, though not many, refuse. The document clearly stipulates that filling in the personal data is not compulsory. It was designed to help the employer become better acquainted with the applicant, so as to regard them on a more personal level.

"If a person objected to providing details of their hobbies and outside interests, Judith wondered why they felt uncomfortable revealing such data about themselves. On the rare occasion when she did hire people who refused to fill in that section, she usually regretted her decision. Not because they did not effectively do their job. Rather, they had difficulties in the area of public relations.

"The pastimes a person engages in away from their occupation has been known to reflect strongly in their job performance. Plus, if they have particular talents in certain areas, we could incorporate those abilities into their job description. It is a way to effectively make use of our human resources. Sometimes, people exhibit expertise in their hobbies. A proficiency we can capitalize on to mutual advantage. Without this section on the application form, we would never learn of such talents."

"There is always the potential for falsifying the data to make a good impression," countered Mel.

"To combat that temptation, Judith asked questions about their choice of hobbies. As you know, your aunt was a well-read lady and possessed extensive knowledge on a number of topics. If the applicant spoke hesitantly on the subject, or gave uninformed responses, she suspected they had fabricated the facts on their application form."

"I didn't realize Judith interviewed the applicants herself. I thought that task would be the responsibility of the department heads."

"Judith had, up to a few months prior to her death, taken an active role in the hiring process. The final selection would be the result of a combined effort. Department heads and Judith met and reviewed the various applications prior to interviews, which all attended. They, then, collectively selected the individual best suited for the job. With her failing health, this duty was delegated to the heads and myself.

"It's funny. When Judith first told me of her method of using the personal data to help in making up her mind about a perspective employee, I laughed at her. I too, wondered what possible bearing one could have on the other. But, after seeing the procedure put into effect, I must admit I find it very beneficial."

"My aunt did tend toward the unorthodox," admitted

Melissa, remembering the many occasions when her aunt's nonconformity became a controversial issue in family discussions.

"It appears you have followed in her footsteps," commented Timothy.

"I never really thought of it that way, but I guess you're right. Even in school I rarely succumbed to peer pressure, preferring to do things my own way, if at all. I always have been a bit of a loner. A trait inherited from my father."

"An admirable man, no doubt."

"Many thought so."

"Perhaps we should check the personnel files to see if they reveal any of the traits Mrs. Newton described. It would be best to do so after the others have left for the day, so as not to invite suspicion on the part of our prey."

"Yes, we should be cautious. If those involved feel we are getting too close, they may feel threatened and become dangerous. We do not want to disintegrate any advantage we have."

"No. More importantly, I have no desire to meet a similar fate as Mark Dunn. If our thief is the one responsible for his murder, he means business."

"You can say that again." Mel shivered at the memory of the condition in which they had discovered Mark.

Their arrival at the office preceded that of Officer Rawlins by a thirty minute interval, long enough to grab soup and sandwiches from the cafeteria and take it to Timothy's office where they ate.

Their meal completed, the secretary announced the detective's arrival. Mike was directed, by Timothy, to Mark's immediate supervisor, Jeffrey Marsh. Mel's hopes to accompany the policeman during his interrogation were thwarted by Mike's insistence that he question the people alone.

"Company rules, ma'am. We can't permit civilians to be present during a murder investigation. Besides, employees tend to clam up if the boss is around."

As expected, Mike asked Marsh the reason behind Mark's

departure from the company. Rawlins, upon learning the man was fired, wanted to know why an employee, with the work record of Mr. Dunn, would be relieved of service.

"You will have to speak with Ms. Carson about that. She wanted him out of here and, as usual, she got her way. I'm sure she will show no sorrow at his passing." The man was obviously distressed over the news of Mark's death. "I shouldn't have said that. I have no right." Despite his own sorrow, the man knew he had been unjust in making assumptions about someone else's emotions. For all he knew, she may have regretted her decision. But, being who she was, was incapable of admitting an error in judgment.

"Did Mr. Dunn have many friends here?" asked Mike. "People he associated with, outside of the work environment."

Mike continued his questioning of the supervisor, though he found himself bewildered as to why Ms. Sommers had failed to inform him of Ms. Carson's participation in Dunn's departure from the agency. Knowing there was no love lost between the two women, he was confused as to the possible motivation behind Melissa's withholding of that particular detail. It was hard to imagine Melissa trying to protect her cousin from possible prosecution. Mike was anxious to hear her explanation for withholding the information. He was certain it would be entertaining, if nothing else.

Mike wished he felt the same about the interview he would have to conduct with the obnoxious Ms. Carson. He had never previously met such a stunningly beautiful woman as Suzanne. It was a shame her personality did not match her looks.

Mr. Marsh's answer to his preceding query, interrupted the detective's musing. "Mark was a popular fellow, liked by almost everybody. I don't remember him being particularly close to anyone at the agency, though. You may get more help, along that line, from some of the other messengers." Mr. Marsh provided the list of the names of those under his supervision.

"Thank you, sir," said Mike. "You have been very helpful."

"You'll make them pay for what they did to him, won't

you?" The statement was more a demand than a question.

"That we will, sir," guaranteed Mike.

"Thank you, Officer. I sure did like that young man."

Noticing the tears in the older man's eyes, the policeman promptly vacated, leaving Marsh alone to deal with his grief. He would need some time to compose himself, before the people under his charge returned.

Those who occupy managerial positions are not often thought of as compassionate people. Rawlins had found this, in many cases, to be an unfair and unjustified assumption. Given the opportunity, they displayed as much emotion as anyone, with a heart.

Speaking of hearts, Mike's next obligatory stop was to visit the woman who gave no indication of having one, Suzanne Carson.

18

"Ms. Carson," the secretary announced, "there is a Detective Rawlins here to see you."

"Tell him I am busy. He will have to come back later."

"I don't believe he really wants to hear that, Ma'am."

"Fine, Gloria, send him in." Suzanne spoke with agitation, quickly placing the nail polish remover into the desk drawer. She picked up a file, in a feeble attempt to appear as busy as she had implied herself to be.

The woman's recovery from the previous evening's news had been miraculous. Most people would have interpreted her prompt emotional recuperation as lack of genuine concern for anyone other than herself. Suzanne was unaware of any such defect in her personality. She preferred to credit her resilience to strength of character.

Fortunately for her, the visitors had presumed her display of emotion was caused by sorrow over the man's passing. Suzanne felt no sorrow over the demise of Mark Dunn. Not that she wanted him dead. Even though he certainly had been creating a good deal of disruption in her life, by his mere existence. She had to admit, however, his removal eliminated potential problems for her.

Considering the last conversation with her lover, Suzanne could have foreseen the inevitability of Mark's death. But, having not directly participated in the murder, she was, at least in her own mind, barren of guilt.

Despite the reassurance she gave herself, she knew she must remain calm when answering the detective's questions. Exercising caution, so as not to hint of any connection between herself and the probable murderer.

"Sorry to interrupt your busy day," apologized Mike. It never failed to amaze him how the people who claim to be overworked, seldom appear so.

"What can I do for you, Detective?" began Suzanne. "As you can see, I am very busy."

"Yes, I can see that. A helpful hint, if I may: you might find it easier to get through the file, if it were not upside down."

"Thank you, Detective. But I'm sure I would have noticed that, once I began reading it."

"I am investigating the murder of a young man formerly employed as a messenger with this agency. One Mark Dunn. You wouldn't know anything about that would you, Miss?"

"Afraid not. Other than being advised of his death, I am totally in the dark. He was merely a former employee. My only association with him was within the confines of this agency."

"I understand you were the person responsible for ordering his dismissal. May I ask why you felt such an action was necessary?"

"He was relieved of duty due to insubordination."

"What type of behavior had he displayed?"

"Insubordination is a fairly straight forward term, Detective. His general attitude was unacceptable. He made several sexual overtures in my direction and showed little respect for my authority."

"I see. So, in essence, what you are saying is that Mr. Dunn displayed a different side of his personality toward you than what was exhibited to the remainder of the staff here."

"Actually, my position comes under the heading of management, Detective. Staff are the people under me. I think that was part of the problem. He could not accept a woman giving him orders."

"I'm a bit confused. Wasn't Mr. Marsh his immediate supervisor? That being so, why would it be necessary for you to have contact with him? Surely any instructions you had for the messenger would have been relayed to him, via Mr. Marsh?"

"That is essentially true. There were a few occasions, however, when I dealt with the young man personally."

"Do you have any idea why he behaved as he did toward you? It hardly fits his image."

"I know he was popular here and am also at a loss to explain why he acted as he did in my presence. Nonetheless, Detective, that is the way it was."

"Is there anyone I could talk to who witnessed this conduct?"

"No, my secretary was out of the office on those occasions. Normally, if she were at her desk, he left the mail with her. When she was out, he had been instructed to deliver the items directly to me."

"Do you have any idea who would want him dead?"

"None, whatsoever."

"Were you aware of the scheduled meeting between Ms. Sommers, Mr. Hudson and the descendent?"

"They told me of the meeting, when they came to the house last evening with news of his murder. That is the first I had heard of it."

"Fine, ma'am, that will be all. For now. If you think of anything which could shed some light on this case, please get in touch with me immediately."

"Yes, Detective. I will be sure to do that."

"Thank you for your time. I know it is precious." Suzanne noticed the sarcastic tone in the man's voice, though chose to ignore it.

After finishing his interview with Suzanne, Rawlins next approached Melissa. "Miss," he began, "why didn't you tell me that it was Ms. Carson who ordered Mr. Dunn's removal from this agency? I was under the impression, after speaking with you last evening, the man's departure was voluntary. Now I learn that was not the case."

"Sorry, sir. Merely an oversight, I assure you." Mel's answer lacked conviction. She knew it. More importantly, so did Rawlins.

"I guess that is the only possible explanation. After all, you would have no reason to protect your cousin."

"None, whatsoever, Detective."

"By the way, I have just come from a chat with the indomitable lady herself. Is she always so disagreeable, or does she exaggerate it for my benefit? If so, she needn't bother."

"That is Suzanne's way with everyone. Actually, I think she is very insecure and uses the bravado as a cover."

"If so, it is one hell of a cover," remarked Mike.

"Did she tell you anything which could be useful?"

"If she did, it was definitely unintentional. She denied any knowledge of, or participation in, the murder, other than learning about it from you and Mr. Hudson last evening.

"Something bugs me about her recollection of the behavior Dunn displayed which caused her to fire him. You see, Miss, I know people. You have to, in my business. A man does not, normally, behave in a manner totally foreign to his basic nature. No one I have spoken to about Dunn had anything but praise for his work and his conduct. No one, that is, other than Ms. Carson. I find that strange, really strange. It just doesn't jive. A man who is well respected among his peers and superiors would not be apt to behave so abominably toward a woman, simply because she occupies a managerial position.

"Another thing that disturbs me is lack of supporting evidence. No one, not even her secretary, saw any proof of her allegations."

"She says her secretary was out of the office when these visits occurred," supplied Melissa.

"Yes, so she told me. Mighty convenient."

"My thoughts, exactly," agreed Mel.

"According to Dunn's previous work record, he was under a woman's direction before. There was no hint of inappropriate conduct. She said she was sorry to lose him. He resigned his post with her company when he received a better offer from this agency."

"Well," commented Melissa, "Suzanne does tend to bring out the worst in people."

"Really, I never would have noticed." Mike chuckled.

"My instincts tell me she is lying about the whole thing. She keeps looking at you when she speaks, almost as if she knows you are not falling for her story."

"I agree. I get the feeling this is going to be one of those weird ones."

"Detective Rawlins, there is something I should advise you of." After discussing the matter with Timothy, the two agreed to inform the policeman of the present difficulties at the agency. The possible link between those events and Mark Dunn's murder could not be ignored. Therefore, the detective should be made aware.

Following Melissa's disclosure, Mike commented, "I tend to agree with you. The incidents must be connected. If only because there seems little other motive for the young man's murder. If someone knew you were planning to meet with him to learn what, if anything, he knew about the embezzlement scheme, and feared he could implicate them, they may have wished to eliminate the possibility of that occurring. Sounds like a good place to start. I just wish you had told me of this sooner."

"Sorry. We had hoped to keep the agency's trouble a secret, as much as possible. However, if that young man was killed because of this business, we have no right to withhold anything which could be of significance to your investigation."

"Thank you, Miss, for your honesty. Do you think the trouble here has anything to do with your aunt's death?"

"I'm not sure. I don't think we should overlook the possibility. Have you learned any more about Aunt Judith's murder?"

"Not yet. I am hoping something will break soon."

"Thanks. Good day, Detective."

"Good day, Miss."

The remainder of the afternoon passed uneventfully. As expected Simon Jennings was elated over the news of his confirmed innocence.

Timothy worked late several evenings a week. Therefore his presence at the office, after the remainder of the staff had left for the day, did not attract attention. When they felt certain the building was empty, the cleaning staff not due for a couple of hours, the amateur sleuths entered the accounting department to study the files of the two male employees.

Though the files were extensive, they failed to provide the type of information the two were hoping to find. Mel was surprised to discover that the files contained photos of both men and their accompanying signatures. "I had forgotten about that," admitted Timothy.

At first overjoyed at this breakthrough, their exhilaration was short-lived. Neither of the signatures even faintly resembled the forger's handwriting. Mrs. Newton had taught them that, even when a person is forging a signature, they may, unconsciously, have a tendency to revert to some of their own writing style. Although the likeness shown would be very subtle, with careful observation, it could usually be detected. Unfortunately, this technique was useless, as it was clear neither of these men were responsible for the forgeries, unless they were more proficient than even the expert had given them credit for.

"I guess that would have been too easy" remarked Melissa, unable to hide her disappointment.

"I still think this is where we should focus our search. Someone had to have access to this section, in order to pull the swindle off. I go with the idea that one of the people working in this area granted our thief entry."

"We should try to find out which of the other employees are close friends with the various members of the accounting personnel."

"You're right. We had best get started."

"Slave driver," teased Mel.

Frustrated at their failure to learn anything useful from the files, the presence of a young man lurking in the shadows went unnoticed. If Melissa had spotted him, she may have recognized the man as the same individual whom she had seen speaking with Suzanne in the hallway, outside of the creative department, a few days earlier.

19

The Carsons were enjoying supper at the mansion, their meal interspersed with tidbits of conversation revolving, predominantly, around business matters.

"Suzanne, why is Katherine still managing the estate's affairs?" asked Donald. "I thought you were planning to fire her. You said she was becoming difficult. What changed your mind?"

"I gave her a stern warning and she promised me she would be easier to get along with. I considered getting some-one else, but she knows our needs and it would take a while to train a new person. Since neither of us has the time to take care of the estate affairs ourselves, it makes more sense to keep her on." Suzanne hoped her speech was convincing. She did not want her brother to learn that keeping Katherine on staff was not her idea. The witch had threatened her with blackmail. Threatened her!

One would think the woman would have been satisfied with the money left her in the will. Not her. She wanted more. Mind you, the will would be in probate for months yet. It would take that long to prove Melissa's invalid claim to the agency. Maybe, when everything was settled, Suzanne could get rid of Katherine, for good. Hopefully, before she had reason to reveal what she knew. Until then, Suzanne would have to tread softly, doing nothing to provoke the woman. This included continuation of the woman's present salary. An excessive amount. Much more than other individuals, with similar posts, were receiving and far more than Katherine deserved.

"Do you have any idea who is responsible for the embezzlement scheme?" Suzanne broached the subject which would effectively take her brother's mind off of Katherine and her continued presence at the estate.

Suzanne had not entirely ruled out the possibility that Donald was involved himself. After all, he had mentioned creating some problems which Mel would be forced to handle. This present situation may be an example of what he was referring to.

"No, I have no idea who is involved."

"You wouldn't, by chance, be doing this, hoping to force Melissa to leave."

"Suzanne what are you nattering on about?"

"Remember, when we found out Mel inherited the company, you mentioned creating a few situations which she would have to manage. I thought, perhaps, this was one you had invented."

"Hardly. I would never do something so detrimental to the agency. Besides, the problem started before Mel arrived here."

"The first incident did. Not the second."

"Actually, although the second one was reported after she began working here, it, too, was in effect before that time."

"You're right. I hadn't thought of that."

"That is one of your big problems. You make too many assumptions without thinking. If you wanted to know, why didn't you just ask me?"

"Because, dear brother, you have been in a foul mood lately. Plus, with Connie away, you are hardly ever home after supper."

"I know and I do not plan to stick around tonight, either."

"Where are you spending all your time? If I didn't know better, I'd think you were having an affair."

"Honestly, Suzanne." Donald shook his head. "Anyway, it looks as though we will not have to invent any phony problems for Melissa. She has her hands full with the real thing."

"Do you think they still believe we are involved?"

"I think they are convinced you are. Remember, you were the one who was originally faced with the initial discrepancies and chose to ignore them. Though why, I will never know. You must admit, that was an incredibly stupid thing to do. What were you thinking about, anyway?"

"Believe me, you don't want to know."

"Try me."

"It is irrelevant now. I gathered it to be a simple case of duplicate ordering and that Jennings was getting distraught over nothing."

"Come now, Suzanne. You have known that man as long as I have. Have you ever known him to over dramatize a situation?"

"Never. But there is always the first time."

"I certainly hope you exercise more wisdom in future."

Suzanne prayed her brother would never learn of her knowledge of the person responsible for the first case of theft. The fact that she was unaware of her lover's participation, until well after she received Simon's report, would carry little weight with Donald. He was sure to stress how wrong she had been, getting involved with such a man in the first place, and how she should have turned him in.

As for the current difficulty, maybe her friend was not involved. Perhaps he had learned from the previous episode. Then again, perhaps not.

Suzanne hated the idea of keeping things from her brother. Although a five-year age gap existed between them, the two had always been able to communicate on a satisfactory level.

Donald, bothered by Suzanne's tendency (ironically one shared by his wife) of putting far too much emphasis on money and social status, tried to overlook those distasteful traits in his sister.

There were times, however, such as during the reading of their mother's will, when her behavior was impossible to condone or ignore. In some ways their personalities were similar (unavoidable since they were related), but in the areas where they differed, the gap was immense.

Donald, married with children, had developed a maturity his sister lacked. Though he no longer found his marriage a satisfying one, it had succeeded in making him more responsible. Actually the children had been the stabilizing influence in his life, not his self-centered wife.

Retrospectively, Donald was unsure what had drawn him to Connie (she preferred Constance, a name he abhorred and refused to address her by). Why, on earth, would a man be attracted to a woman who possessed all the negative qualities he found so repulsive in his sister? The only answer he could derive was that he had been blinded by her beauty and apparent interest in him.

As he had often heard people say—men are seldom ruled by their heads in matters of love and sexual attraction. Women, on the other hand, know what they want and go out and get it. They rarely allow such a trivial thing as sex to detract them from their ultimate goal. What the driving force was behind their selection, he did not know. The only thing of which he was certain was they were not governed by the same primal urges as men.

"Have you any idea who was responsible for the original theft?" asked Donald.

"Not a clue."

"Well, if you do, you would be wise to reveal it. People have ways of finding out facts we believe are safely hidden." Donald was unconvinced of his sister's claim of ignorance in the caper, so thought it best to warn her of the possible ramifications of such involvement.

"I'll remember that," replied Suzanne. "Don't be concerned about me. I can look after myself."

"I'll remind you of that when you come running to me to bail you out of the next predicament you find yourself in." Neither realized just how quickly Donald's words would become reality.

"Well, you are my brother. You should instinctively come to my aid with, or without, my plea for help." Suzanne was applying her "put on a pout" expression: this look so labeled by the very individual now on the receiving end of it.

"I feel an obligation to do so, to a point, Suzanne. However, your need to avail yourself of my 'knight in shining armor' services have occurred with a fair degree of regularity, as of late, don't you agree? When you were younger, you got yourself into trouble because of the crowd you hung around with. Now you are older, though no more selective in choosing your friends. The only thing that has changed is the severity of the plights you find yourself drawn into, through those associations."

"You have never approved of my friends," accused Suzanne.

"No, I must agree with you there. Did you ever think I may have had a valid reason for my disapproval of the people you choose to spend time with? Most of your so-called friends enjoy the pleasure of your company, because, and only because, they enjoy the company of your wealth. If the money disappeared, so would they. I don't know why you can't see that." Donald inwardly scolded himself for being drawn into this debate. A discussion which had been ongoing since childhood. He did not like, nor trust, Suzanne's companions. He did not approve of people using others for their personal gain. The only rationale which would explain Suzanne's choice of companions was that people tended to associate with their own kind.

"As usual, you are exaggerating. Just because you are willing to mingle with those beneath you, you needn't put me down for failing to do the same. I prefer to spend time with individuals who have similar breeding to myself." Suzanne's facial expression was as smug as her statement.

"I swear you must have been a thoroughbred horse in a previous life. I just wish you could hear yourself. When you talk in that manner I am embarrassed to admit we are related."

Before Suzanne could respond to Donald's stingy retort (a reply which would surely have precipitated a rather heated argument), Carmelita entered the room to announce Detective Rawlins' arrival.

"Detective, good evening," greeted Donald, relieved by the interruption. "Have you had any luck with the investigation into Mother's murder?"

"Sorry to disturb you folks, but that is precisely why I am here. We found this can of rat poison which, by the way, contains a high concentration of arsenic, in the garbage cans just outside the stables. Do either of you know how it got there?"

"We used to have some trouble with rats around the stables. Mr. Conrad must have used the poison to dispose of the problem. Why don't you ask him, as that is his domain?"

"We did, sir. He told us he never saw the can before. He also said he would never use poison around the horses, for fear they would accidentally ingest it. In fact, sir, he said the problem had been taken care of months ago, after he adopted a couple of barn cats."

"Mr. Conrad tends to be forgetful," volunteered Suzanne. "He may have used it before he got the cats and it slipped his mind. If it wasn't for his ability with the horses and his close friendship with Mother, he would have been relieved of service months ago. You must have noticed his advanced years for a man employed in his position."

"Perhaps he did use it to get rid of the rats," suggested Donald. "Maybe he became frightened when he learned that arsenic was used to poison Mother and discarded the can, realizing someone must have known it was there and borrowed it. He probably feared he would be blamed for not being more careful."

"I will check into the possibility. If he were lying, he does a damn fine job. He looked as surprised as we, when my partner found the can.

"In the meantime, it does provide us with a probable source for the arsenic. We will dust the can for prints and will let you know what we find.

"Goodnight folks. I'll see myself out."

"The plot thickens. This man seems to know his business."

Donald spoke with admiration for the detective's apparent competence. The look his statement evoked from his sister hardly qualified as admiration. Rather, more aptly described as fear.

20

Melissa and Timothy left the office, tired and discouraged. Each trying, unsuccessfully, to hide their feelings of frustration from the other. The prospects of a hot bath and commencement of a new mystery novel were the only incentives driving Melissa onward.

As she left the parking lot the light rain which had started (in protest to the weather person's prediction) by early afternoon, had increased in intensity. Mel minded night driving. Her dislike of the activity intensified with the addition of precipitation to lessen visibility and make the experience more dangerous. In such circumstances, she slackened her speed appreciably, a reaction she was soon to be eternally grateful for.

The moment she reached town limits, Mel adjusted the car's headlights to the brighter mode. She advanced cautiously, to avoid hydroplaning (a hazard created by the pools of water which had accumulated). Approximately two miles out of town, slowing to negotiate a particularly treacherous curve in the road, Mel was concerned over the lack of response received through her habit of gently pumping the brakes. She found this method superior to an abrupt reduction in speed brought about by applying the brakes too firmly, especially on wet or slippery pavement.

Attributing the decreased brake function to dampness, she calmly repeated the pumping action, which resulted in a similar response, or lack thereof. Panic was a reaction Melissa had learned, through her nurses training, to curtail. It tends to interfere with one's mental processes. The best approach was a calm assessment of the situation. Calm, but expedient.

Of paramount importance was finding alternate means for slowing the vehicle's forward motion. The most obvious technique to employ would be careful utilization of the handbrake and gearing down the manual transmission while saying a short prayer (never a wasted exercise when faced with an emergency, provided one kept it concise). In this instance, Melissa deemed, "Please, help me God!" to be sufficient, she gently applied the parking brake. Due to her curtailed speed, strategic employment of a damaged handbrake, gearing down the five speed transmission and, most of all, the prayer for heavenly intervention, Melissa was able to bring the vehicle to a halt. When she insured the car was completely and safely parked, Melissa began to tremble. A thoroughly normal and beneficial reaction to stress. Melissa deduced that a brush with death (a distinct possibility had she been unable to stop the vehicle), would qualify as stress.

When her trembling ceased, Melissa evaluated the dilemma she found herself in. She had successfully brought the car to a halt at the side of the road, thus eliminating the danger of damage to her vehicle by oncoming traffic.

The prospect of walking in the rain, though unpleasant,

was preferable to remaining with the vehicle, especially as Melissa was cold and weary. She was aware that the first rule of traffic safety is to remain with the vehicle. Usually one to obey such guidelines, Melissa was tempted, on this occasion, to ignore the advice. She did not relish the prospect of waiting for someone to come along to offer assistance. The road was, after all, deserted. With the nasty weather, the wait could be a lengthy one. Mel feared the likelihood of an individual stopping, who had less than honorable intentions in mind, was a strong probability.

As the inn was only a few miles down the road, Mel considered two other options. She could walk the remaining distance in the rain, without an umbrella (having not foreseen any need to bring one). Or, she could continue driving her disabled automobile with a good deal of caution, at a speed strongly resembling a crawl.

When the intensity of the rain suddenly took on a torrential quality, her decision became one of practicality. She was too tired to face the challenge of a two mile walk in a downpour and, if someone wished to do her bodily harm, she was too easily accessible if walking. Wisely interpreting the suddenly intensified storm as a heavenly hint, Melissa opted for driving the short stretch to the inn.

The danger was reduced by absence of any hills or further turns in the road, the route to the inn being straight and fairly level. She acknowledged the percentage of brake function remaining, and drove accordingly. Her progress, while steady, was indeed crab-like.

The lights of the inn, once in her field of vision, were akin to a beacon guiding her onward. By the time she deposited herself and the vehicle at their destination, Melissa had become rather adept at maneuvering a motorized auto, with only a malfunctioning handbrake as a means of curtailing her speed. A newly discovered aptitude she had no desire to retest any time in the near, or distant, future.

Refusing to take time to reflect on what had just transpired, Mel promptly went to the dining room, not so much for the eagerly awaited dinner, as for the cup of hot tea accompanying it. The beverage proved soothing to her heightened senses. Though unaccustomed to drinking tea with a hefty amount of sugar, Mel felt the situation called for precisely that.

Upon returning to her room, Melissa indulged in the anticipated hot bath. She found it equally comforting. How much more enjoyable simple pleasures became, after one has faced imminent peril and possible removal of those pleasures forever.

With restoration of her equilibrium, Melissa contemplated the incident. Recalling her recent three month routine checkup on the car (which had revealed no defects or hint of mechanical malfunctioning), the possibility of the brake failure being accidental could be all but eliminated. The only other explanation was tampering. Only one question remained. Who?

A telephone call Mel received a short time later confirmed her suspicions. To her "Hello," an angry male voice responded, "Did you enjoy your adventure? Next time you will not get off so easy.

Leave town, or suffer the consequences!" The caller disconnected, before Mel had time to respond to his intimidation.

"Well, I guess that removes any possibility of the brakes letting go accidentally," said Melissa, speaking aloud. She hoped, by doing so, to decrease the tachycardia her heart was presently experiencing.

Following his call to Melissa, the young man accessed a private line at the mansion. "She is still alive. I left her handbrake partially connected, as promised. I gave her a warning. She is to leave town while she has a chance."

"Remember," his partner replied, "you promised that murder was a weapon to be used only as a last resort. There has been enough killing."

"Fine, but I am not a very patient person. If I see no sign that she is leaving, we will have to employ a more permanent means of persuasion." The man was willing to concur with the woman's restrictions, to a point. If the desired results could be achieved without resorting to violence, so be it. If they were unsuccessful, he had no qualms about removing any and all obstacles.

The elimination of Mark Dunn had been almost too easy. There wasn't even a struggle. Mark had accepted his explanation as to why he had paid the visit. Just to check up on him and see how he was doing, the man had explained. Having been friends when both worked at the agency, Mark had no reason to suspect the man had been the one behind his dismissal or that he would wish him harm.

Mark had been stupid to turn his back on him. God, he hated stupid people. That is why he had to do something about Suzanne. Her stupidity could cost him everything.

Not to worry. When the police discovered her fingerprints on the tire iron which had been used to bash in Dunn's skull, Ms. Carson would no longer pose a problem. She would have difficulty talking her way out of that one. Especially when they established that she was the only one with a motive. He knew she would not mention their connection. Fear would silence her tongue. She knew what he would do to her if she squealed.

He had thought of everything. All that remained was to dispose of Melissa Sommers. He hoped she would heed his warning and leave town. But, if she chose not to take his advice, that was her choice. She would have to suffer the consequences of such an unwise decision. Again, that would be stupid.

And to think, Mama had always called him stupid. He had shown Mama. Her elimination had been easy too. A heart attack they had called it.

Drugs were wonderful solutions to problems. Mama had always been a problem. Now, Mama was gone. No one had suspected murder. Why would they? Mama and he had always been so close. He was devastated by her death. That was their interpretation. God, they were stupid.

Once Melissa was taken care of the man would reconsider

his options. He was well acquainted with the spending potential of his accomplice. Her substantial inheritance would not last as long as it would in the hands of a more discriminating consumer, such as himself. Having control of a multi-million dollar advertising company was a different matter. It would take, even her, a while to dispose of that amount of capital. The most encouraging outlook: the funds would be constantly replenished, as opposed to receiving one lump sum.

After they married and he insured her will named him sole benefactor, an accident could then be arranged, leaving him with everything. One thing would be missing. Her constant nagging. And that, he could comfortably do without. Just as he had managed, quite nicely, without Mama's.

Replacing her in his bed should not pose a problem, bearing in mind the sizable entourage he could now boast. Some, though not many, of the offers for sexual fulfillment directed toward him, had been rejected. He had been discriminating. It would not be prudent to engage in extracurricular activities with women who were known to publicly broadcast their conquests. This used to be a custom engaged in only by the male of the species. Another change wrought by liberation. Women now, on occasion, treated men as trophies too.

His associate could hardly oppose all of his sexual exploits. It was through such an encounter that they had obtained a copy of the key to the accounting department of Carson Agency. The fact that she was oblivious to the ongoing liaison with his unwitting and unintentional ally was a trivial matter. He did not deny their association. If she asked him, he would tell her. She just never asked.

Melissa was, at that moment, feeling the effects of the evening's events. She wanted consolation. Ironically, she automatically thought of Timothy. Having known him for such a short period of time, it disturbed her that he was the first person who came to mind when she needed a shoulder.

His opening remark, upon hearing her commentary on the night's experience, was to ask her if she required chauffeur services for the morning. Mel was shocked by what she considered to be an unsuitable reaction to her ordeal. "I must say, you get to the root of a problem quickly," she said, her tone brusque. "To be honest, that was not my primary concern."

"Sorry, Melissa. That was callous of me. It is a nasty habit of mine to evaluate a situation through listing priorities. Mobility seemed to rank as number one."

"Funny, I don't quite see it that way. Preserving my life, was number one on my list of things to do. So silly of me." Mel's tone remained curt. "Sorry to disturb you with such a trivial matter. You needn't fret over my lack of transportation. I will hitch a ride with the tow truck in the morning. Goodnight." Saying this, Melissa replaced the receiver, none too gently, into its cradle.

The action reminded her that she had overlooked one little detail. She had neglected to inform the police of her adventure. Although there was probably little they could do, whoever had tampered with her brakes undoubtedly having worn gloves, she still must make the effort.

Following answering the barrage of questions directed toward her, Melissa informed the officer of the garage where she would be leaving the car. Expressing to the policeman the degree of fatigue she felt, she stated her preference that he inspect the vehicle the next day at the garage, rather than visit her that evening. At first verbalizing disapproval of putting off the inspection, he finally relented, only after receiving her guarantee that she would advise the mechanic not to touch the vehicle until a police officer could examine it.

Though the policeman offered her protection, she promptly declined. He encouraged her to call again if there was a repeat of the message or any further sign of harassment. It was apparent that he questioned her wisdom in refusing assistance, clearly stating that it was her decision and he could not force her to accept protection. Melissa promised the officer she would notify him, if anything untoward happened.

To prevent any repeat telephone threats, Mel took the phone off the hook and settled down to begin reading the novel

21

Melissa was awakened by a rap on the door. Momentarily forgetting where she was (having been aroused from a deep sleep), her first instinct was to look at the clock. It was only ten P.M. Noticing the book at her side, she remembered starting the first chapter. She must have drifted off. Understandable, considering how tired she had been. Reading usually made her sleepy, even when she felt no fatigue prior to beginning the activity.

She could hear Mrs. Wilson's voice calling out, "Melissa, dear. Are you all right?"

"Yes, Mrs. Wilson, I am fine." Melissa responded.

"There is someone here to see you. Should I ask him to come back at a more convenient time?"

Donning her bathrobe, Melissa went to the door. She opened it to the expected sight of Mrs. Wilson and the unexpected presence of Timothy Hudson. "I tried calling you and kept getting a busy signal." The young man explained. "I was a bit worried. Okay, I was a lot worried."

"Are you sure you are okay, Melissa?" repeated Mrs. Wilson.

"Yes. I started reading and fell asleep."

"Is it all right for this young man to visit or would you prefer he come back at another time?"

"No, he can stay. That is, if you have no objection? It is getting late for visitors."

"No problem, my dear. He looks like a respectable young fellow. He may stay as long as you wish." Mrs. Wilson departed, Melissa noticing the admiring glances her landlady cast in Timothy's direction.

"I must apologize for my insensitivity," Timothy began. "You were probably scared out of your wits, as anyone would have been. Do you have any idea who tampered with your car?"

"Timothy, why don't you come in," offered Melissa, relishing the fact that he was the one who was now less than composed. "It is difficult to conduct a conversation, with you standing in the doorway.

"Do you care for a coffee? Mrs. Wilson kindly permits the use of a coffee percolator in my room. I drink a fair bit of the brew and the dining room is only open during meal times."

"She seems like a nice lady," said Timothy, as he entered the room. "A coffee would be great, but an answer to my question would be even better."

"I've done nothing else but answer questions. The police had a rather long list of them. In response to yours, no, I have no idea. The voice of the caller was definitely male, youthful and sufficiently threatening."

"He made reference to the disturbance with your brakes."

"Not only did he refer to it, he took credit for the action. He also implied that, next time, I might not be so lucky. Apparently he deliberately provided me with a partially functional handbrake."

"How could he be certain you would have thought to apply the emergency brake to slow the vehicle? The average person would panic, not thinking to employ that means of slowing the vehicle. Or, if they did, would be apt to use it improperly, which can be equally as dangerous."

"I'm glad you didn't say most women would panic. If you had, I would have been tempted to scream. I really don't think the man particularly cared, one way or the other. By leaving me with some braking function, he gave me a sporting chance. It was up to me whether or not I capitalized on it."

"How, may I ask, do you propose to prevent further incidents? Do you plan to leave town, as requested?"

"It was hardly a request and I do not react well to threats. The police offered me protection, which I refused."

"What do you mean, you refused?" Timothy, could not believe what he was hearing.

"Just what I said. If this person thinks I am going to tuck my tail between my legs and silently steal away, he is sadly mistaken. I am in this for the long haul. He has warned me and I will be careful. Aside from that, my game plan is unchanged.

"When I started this assignment, I did so to fill the void left by Judith's death, until such time as a suitable replacement could be found. Unless, of course, I choose to carry on myself in the capacity of general manager. My other motivation was to find out who killed her. I have no intention of leaving here until that mystery is solved."

"Do you think your life is being threatened because of our investigation?"

"No. I think it is more likely connected with Judith's death. Whoever wanted her out of the way, probably desires my removal for the same reason. They want Carson Agency and I am standing in their way of getting it. With me gone, the final obstacle would be effectively disposed of."

"So you believe your cousins are instrumental in what happened to you tonight?"

"I can think of no one else who fits the bill. Judith's house staff was handsomely provided for in her will. Their jobs are intact, her children having made no alterations to date. They would have no reason to assume they would receive any more, or any less. Judith, as usual, was more than generous."

"Is it possible that Donald or Suzanne could have commissioned the services of one of the staff in their mother's removal?" suggested Timothy.

"Possible, though highly unlikely. Judith had a close friendship with all of her staff. I don't believe any of them would help to dispose of her. Besides, considering the obnoxious way Suzanne treated them, I doubt if they would help her do anything their job description did not demand.

"Poisoning is not a violent act, in the truest sense of the word. Therefore, someone not prone to violence could justify the deed and carry it out, without assistance from others.

"There is also the possibility of hiring out for murder. If you have enough money. That may be the route they are taking to insure my removal."

"Aren't you being a bit lax in your attitude toward this threat? It matters little if they 'hire out', as you so tactfully put it, or if they carry out the act themselves. The outcome for you is the same. Dead is dead."

"You have an excellent grasp of the obvious," stated Melissa.

"This is not something to joke about. Your life is in danger. I'm sure that was not what Judith had in mind, when she left you the company."

"Timothy, I will not allow a few scare tactics to frighten me away."

"But we are talking about murder," stressed Timothy, convinced the woman was becoming unglued. "For all we know, this may be the same person who disposed of Mark Dunn. Quite effectively, I might add. I have no wish to see you left in the same state."

"I know that, and I have no desire to meet the same fate he did. You must admit, if the roles were reversed, you would feel the same way. You would not allow someone to frighten you away."

"But I am a..."

"Don't even say it!" interrupted Mel. "The fact that you are a man is irrelevant."

"But I can defend myself more easily."

"Really. You are forgetting one thing."

"What is that?"

"Mark Dunn was a man. It certainly did not protect him. Besides, my being a woman may be a positive thing."

"How so?"

"Perhaps the killer likes women and has some aversion to doing away with me, unless it is totally necessary. If I had been a man, he may have been tempted to disconnect my brakes entirely."

"Let's hope you are right. I would hate to see anything happen to you. You make a pretty good boss."

"Is that all?" asked Melissa, suggestively. Astonished at the words escaping her lips.

"No," answered Timothy, as he gently kissed her cheek. "But that is all I will admit for now and it is a grand place to start. Goodnight, sleep well. I will pick you up in the morning to drive you to the office."

"I'll be ready." Melissa was disappointed to see Timothy leave, though acknowledged the wisdom in his decision to do so. She was in a vulnerable state. Something no real gentleman would take advantage of.

22

Despite her brave declaration, Melissa spent a fitful night. The reason for her restlessness was simple: she was scared. Timothy was right. Endangering her life was not something Judith would have included in the agreement.

Some danger was expected. The very fact that Mel had inherited the agency did not sit well with several individuals. But who would demonstrate their displeasure in a violent form?

And, if Judith had been aware of the embezzlement scheme, why had she not warned her niece? The discussion they had carried out on that last evening had afforded her the perfect opportunity to do so. But she had not mentioned it. Why?

Timothy had promised to pick Melissa up at eight-thirty

173

A.M. His arrival coincided with that of the tow truck. The mechanic had informed her that, depending on the extent of the damage and how readily the necessary parts could be obtained, her vehicle may well be incapacitated for several days. She was advised to call later in the morning, at which time they would have had a chance to determine what repairs were needed and how long they would take.

"Don't worry," reassured Timothy. "If the car is not fixed by the end of the day, I will drive you home and pick you up in the morning."

As they drove away Timothy asked, "Do you have any specific plans for today?"

"I thought I would check with Detective Rawlins to see if he is any closer to solving Judith's murder. I also planned to review more employee files in hopes of discovering someone who fits the description we received from Mrs. Newton."

Mel's intended contact with the policeman became superfluous as Donald and Suzanne were waiting to see her when she reached her office, eager to relate the details of the detective's visit to the mansion the previous evening.

"They found a can of rat poison outside the stables," announced Donald. "It contains arsenic. Conrad does not remember seeing the can prior to Mother's death and swears he did not use it. Considering his poor memory, the fact that he cannot recall having seen it before can hardly be accepted as gospel."

"Have they retrieved any fingerprints from the can?" asked Mel.

"No, they hadn't dusted it yet."

"It was probably wiped clean anyway," said Mel. "It is unlikely the person who poisoned Judith would leave fingerprints. Did Rawlins say how they think the arsenic was administered?"

"They removed all dishes from her room and anything which she used exclusively. He did not say what, if anything, they learned form the tests run on the articles." Donald told his cousin what he knew. "I suspected someone gave it to her in her nightly glass of warm milk. She had not been eating much lately, but continued to enjoy her warm milk before retiring. She said it helped her sleep better. Maybe the person who poisoned her thought it would be a good way to put her to sleep permanently. Since they say she received the lethal dose only a few hours prior her death, that is the only way she could have ingested it."

"Why don't you tell them that and they can arrest the person who prepared Mother's milk that evening and we can be finished with all this aggravation," suggested Suzanne.

"I really don't think you want me to do that," said Donald.

"Why not?" asked his sister. "What are you talking about?"

"If memory serves, you were the one who took Mother her warm milk on the fateful evening."

"My God, you're right. I forgot. If they find that out, they will arrest me on the spot. What am I going to do? Donald, you know I could not bear to go to prison."

"Suzanne, calm down. If they had any indication the milk was the method used, they would surely have checked into it by now. The tests must not have shown anything in the milk glass."

"Who usually took Judith her milk?" asked Mel.

"Whoever was the last to retire for the night. She liked to read for several hours before drinking it," explained Donald.

"If that is the case, she must have been given the poison in some other form of food or drink, as she had been receiving it for some time."

"The only problem with that theory is that she ate the same meals as the rest of us and we have displayed no ill effects."

"Was there any other occasion when she ate or drank alone?"

"Her tea," offered Suzanne. "She loved a cup in the afternoon. Since no one else was fond of it, she usually drank it alone."

"Yes. As I remember, Judith was a fussy tea drinker, requiring the teapot be rinsed with boiling water and the tea steeped exactly five minutes. Who prepared it?"

"She was always present when her tea was brewed. Insisted on it. She never trusted us alone with her tea, for fear we would forget and leave it steeping too long." Donald quickly defeated each of Mel's ideas. "Is there any other way she could have received it, other than in her food?"

"Food is the most popular way to give it. Either that, or in her pills. Dr. Adams checked those. They were clean."

"I just wish they could solve this case and leave us alone," stated Suzanne. "All this unpleasantness has interfered with my beauty sleep. The bags under my eyes are becoming increasingly difficult to hide."

Melissa noticed her cousin did not look her usual vibrant self. She would be interested to know how much of Suzanne's lack of rest was due to the police investigation and how much could be attributed to guilt.

"Remember, 'they always get their man'," said Donald, attempting to reassure his sister.

"Somehow, I do not find that particularly comforting. Who is to say when they get their man, they get the right one?"

Suzanne had a point. There had been cases where people had been tried, and convicted, for crimes they did not commit.

After her conversation with her cousins, Melissa met with Timothy. The assistant manager had news. Unpleasant news. He had received two more reports of double billing. They must do something to placate those clients affected. And they had to find a solution soon.

As in the case of Mr. Allen, the second bill was paid prior to investigation. With most companies, this behavior would have been inappropriate. Carson Agency was different. Their outstanding reputation for integrity was what had made the embezzlement scheme work in the first place. Their clients initially failed to question the billing, assuming it was necessary. They had held accounts with Carson Agency for years, always finding them above reproach. This was one occasion when a fine reputation was not a positive thing. It had been used against them.

"You will notice," said Timothy, "the only clients affected

are those with whom we have had prolonged dealings. The thief obviously assumed any new clients would object more strenuously to the extra billing. Unfamiliar with our routine, they would not be aware of the occasional need for us to submit a bill for increased costs."

"We can put it off no longer. We must notify the remaining clients of this situation, reminding them to notify us prior to paying anything of this nature."

"I will construct the memo and have my secretary mail it out."

Melissa decided to notify her contact. Things were rapidly getting out of control and she needed advice as to how to proceed.

23

Raymond Currie was pensive. As Suzanne had declared she would, she had approached various lawyers in regard to contesting Judith's will. As indicated by the letter he had just received, she had found one who had agreed to represent her. His name was James Davis, an attorney noted for accepting the cases most reputable lawyers declined. Where his colleagues advised their potential client of the improbability of success, James would lead them to believe they had a strong case. Suzanne was the type of individual who would be taken in by such a shyster. Not because she was gullible, but because she was desperate. Desperation was more difficult to overcome than sheer stupidity.

Davis relied on the Suzannes of the world for the bulk of

his practice. His conduct, while unethical, could hardly be deemed illegal. On the contrary, the one area where the lawyer was not lacking, was in his knowledge of the law. He knew exactly where the line of legality crossed. Though he had skirted it many times, he had never been proven to cross it, a source of much frustration to Raymond and several of his peers, who wished to put the man out of business. On numerous occasions they thought they had him right where they wanted him only to have him escape their legal clutches.

"One of these days, that man is going to get what is coming to him." Raymond spoke aloud, to a room absent of listeners. "Will I gloat when that day arrives? Just watch me." He slammed the letter down in disgust, deciding it would be best to wait until the morrow to reply. Hopefully, at that time, his anger would have waned, allowing him to construct a polite response. He was incapable of doing so now.

Raymond's discussion with himself was interrupted by an incoming call. He recognized the woman's voice as soon as she spoke, "Melissa, why are you calling me? I thought we agreed only to contact each other if absolutely necessary."

"We did and it is," was the reply. "Don't worry, Ray, I am calling from a pay phone." The fact the matter was serious was evident. Melissa would not have called him, especially at the office, had it not been. "We have to meet to discuss a development at the agency. Timothy and I have been stymied in our attempts to handle it."

"Why don't we meet at the restaurant across the street from my office?" suggested the lawyer. "You go there before me. Then, I'll drop in unexpectedly, so to speak. We can make it appear as if our encounter is totally accidental."

"That should work. I will be there at six o'clock."

"Fine. I'll arrive between six-fifteen and six-thirty. Be careful to give no indication you notice my entrance."

Following the telephone conversation, Ray's thoughts reverted to Suzanne. Raymond knew the woman's wants were many. Though his legal portfolio earned him a sizable annual income, the sum paled in comparison to the wealth Suzanne normally had at her disposal. And, disposing of money was something Suzanne was indeed proficient at. Any romantic overtures on his part were sure to be declined on that point alone.

After dictating several reports, Raymond noticed time had sped by. His secretary announced her departure for the day, bidding him goodnight.

Gladys was an attractive girl and a competent secretary. She had often hinted that she would be receptive to a more personal relationship between them. Raymond had given the idea some thought, but refrained from actively pursuing the prospect. It was unfair to Gladys to indicate an interest in her he did not feel. Until he settled his obsession with Suzanne it was impossible to consider other romantic possibilities. He could not switch his affections so easily.

"God must have an odd sense of humor," he spoke to the empty office, "to activate a man's hormones in the direction of a woman who could only cause him grief."

After reviewing a few more files, Raymond glanced at his watch. It revealed the hour of six o'clock. Time to put away his files and head to the restaurant. Melissa was waiting.

That lady entered the restaurant, surveying the establishment for a private table, though one where Raymond would be sure to see her when he arrived. She ordered a cocktail and perused the menu.

Mel was bothered by the feeling she was being tailed. Timothy had driven her to the garage, where she retrieved her car, after paying the hefty repair bill. The mechanic told her that her brake lines had been cut. The handbrake attached only "by a thread." He was amazed she had escaped a serious accident. Had she been driving at normal speed the handbrake, with its limited function, would have been totally useless.

Melissa was sipping her drink when the lawyer arrived. Taking care not to appear to have noticed his entrance, Mel averted her gaze. Although the restaurant was far from crowded, they must persist in making their encounter appear unplanned.

Raymond played his role superbly, allowing the waiter to

lead him to another table, before slowing his strides as he showed recognition of the woman sitting alone in the corner.

"Ms. Sommers, is that you?" he asked. "Fancy meeting you here. Are you waiting for someone or would you care for some company? Personally, I detest dining alone."

"I was thinking the same thing. Why don't you join me?"

This exchange was staged for the waiter's benefit and anyone who may have overseen their greeting. Raymond ordered a rum and coke, awaiting its arrival before engaging in significant conversation. After ordering their dinners, exchanging a few pleasantries and casual chatter, Mel began to outline the predicament which prompted her call. When she concluded, she asked, "Were you aware of any difficulties the agency was experiencing before Judith's disappearance? Something requiring her intervention."

"She mentioned a slight irregularity, but stated it was under control. The reason I remember is: she told me she was considering possible legal action against those involved. I presumed she had decided it did not merit such action as she never mentioned it again."

"How is she doing, by the way?" This question was innocent enough, Melissa reasoned, as the waiter delivered their meal.

Raymond delayed his response until their waiter was out of hearing distance. "She is fine. Cruising with Dr. Adams has done wonders for her. The effects of the arsenic poisoning have all but vanished. She isn't even using her wheelchair. Adams feels her decreased mobility was a result of the arsenic, more so than her MS."

"When is she due to return?"

"In another week. Unless I notify her that her homecoming will have to be postponed. That is not something I relish having to do. Although she is enjoying the trip, she is anxious to be back in familiar surroundings."

"Was she at her funeral? There was a woman, dressed in black with dark glasses, at the back of the church. I wondered if it was she. If so, she took an awful chance by being there.

What if someone else had seen her and recognized her?"

"I advised her not to go, but she insisted. You can't blame her. What person doesn't want to know how many people would attend their funeral?"

"How did she get in and out so quickly, without her wheelchair?"

"Dr. Adams helped her. She did not stay long. I think you're the only one who even noticed her there."

"Yes, I believe so. I mentioned the figure to a few people. They looked at me as though I was losing my mind. I began to wonder if I were having hallucinations."

"No, your mind is sound. Wish I could say the same for your aunt, taking such a chance. Anyway, do you have any leads in solving this embezzlement threat?"

"No, that is why I came to you, in hopes that Judith had told you about the previous episode and who was responsible. My theory is that she discovered who the culprit was and gave them a stern warning it was not to be repeated. The activity ceased until after her presumed death."

"I cannot see Judith merely warning those responsible. She would be more apt to fire them immediately. Stealing is one thing she has little tolerance for."

"Unless it was one of her children," stated Mel. "That is the only explanation I can come up with. The only person dismissed within the last six months was Mark Dunn, a messenger with the agency, who was murdered the other evening."

"What!" exclaimed Raymond. "This is getting serious."

"You're telling me. We had arranged to meet with him, in regard to the circumstances surrounding his release. He was dead when we got there."

"What do you mean 'the circumstances surrounding his release'?"

"Suzanne fired him, for what she states was inappropriate behavior. It just doesn't jive. He was well respected at the agency and his immediate supervisor had nothing but good things to say about him. The only thing that makes any sense is that he knew Suzanne was behind the embezzlement and threatened to expose her. So she fired him."

"Do you have any proof?" asked Raymond, unable to believe what Melissa was telling him.

"None. If I did, I would be doing more than talking to you about it. She is hiding something, but she refuses to reveal what she knows. Suzanne was the only one who knew we were looking into Mark's discharge. We believe she may have had something to do with his death."

"Melissa, I refuse to believe she could do such a thing. Just as I refuse to believe she tried to kill her mother. I went along with this plan, because it seemed the only way to find out who was poisoning Judith. That has yet to be established. To my knowledge there is no evidence definitely pointing to Suzanne. Until there is, I will not believe she is responsible."

"Raymond, I have sensed, for some time, your feelings toward my cousin. Love tends to blind a person to the faults of the object of their affection."

"Don't worry, Mel. I am all too aware of Suzanne's faults. However, no matter what the motivation may be, I just don't happen to believe they include murder. Don't you think I chastise myself, on a regular basis, for being attracted to such a self-serving, shallow female? My only excuse is that I know there is a kinder, gentler Suzanne, hidden beneath that facade. She is using her cold exterior to conceal a vulnerability she is afraid to reveal."

"God, you are smitten," laughed Mel. "I just hope you are not hurt in your efforts to uncover the warm, gentle side to Suzanne's personality. An element, which if present, is deeply, and I do mean deeply, hidden.

"You are a nice man, Ray. You deserve someone who can love you unselfishly. I'm not sure Suzanne has the ability to do so. Her self-centered attitude is ingrained in every fiber of her being. Has been since childhood. I'm not sure she can turn it off, but I hope, for your sake, she can."

"So do I. Until I convince myself it is not worth the effort, I will continue to try to win her over."

"Good luck, Ray. Perhaps, if you were to reveal your interest, it might make an impression. Giving her a reason to want to change."

"That is what I am counting on. When the time is right, I will tell her how I feel. After the mystery behind the attempted murder of Judith is solved. If I am speaking with your aunt, do you want me to tell her about the problem at the agency?"

"No, it will only worry her. And, she is too far away to do anything about it. If she were to learn there was a problem, she would insist on returning immediately. That would only serve to negate all our efforts in discovering who poisoned her. Timothy and I will just have to work harder to come up with the answers."

"Okay, but let me know if I can be of any help." Raymond neglected to mention the letter from Suzanne's lawyer. Mel had enough to deal with, without that. By the time the case got to court, Judith would be home. Or so he hoped.

As they walked to the exit, Melissa noticed a man sitting alone. He looked familiar, but, for the life of her, she could not remember from where. Before long she was to regret her lack of recall.

24

Melissa's drive to the inn was spent in contemplation. So much so, she failed to observe the vehicle following her.

The man had recognized the individual who had met with Melissa in the restaurant. Despite straining to hear their conversation, he was unable to do so. Perhaps their meeting was as accidental as it appeared. Though he had his doubts.

He decided to tail the woman. Keeping enough distance between them, to avoid making his presence known. Until such time as he had effectively caught her off guard. He did not intend on harming her. At least, not yet. Scaring her was what he had in mind. Letting her know he meant business. Being a relatively intelligent person, she would realize he was the same one who had called. In the darkness, after he dimmed his lights, she would be too startled to get a clear view of his license plate.

Mel felt the nudge. She didn't see the car. With the headlights off, it was almost invisible. The night was so dark. The second bump was stronger. With it, there was an instant flash of bright light. Her loss of control of the steering was momentary, but long enough for the vehicle behind her to speed past without risking identification. Concentrating on regaining control of her car, Melissa could not take the time to observe the plate number of the one which had bumped her.

Pulling to the side of the road to calm herself, Melissa realized she had just experienced another sample of what she had to look forward to. Those people who wanted her out of the way planned to persist in their attack, until she relented or was eliminated.

Mrs. Wilson welcomed her return. In her hand she held a note which she handed to her tenant.

"Someone dropped this off, just a moment ago."

The note was direct and threatening. Its message clear. "Go away or you will be sorry," it read. "I am tired of playing games."

Mrs. Wilson noticed the paleness of Mel's features. "Is anything wrong, dear?

"Who delivered this?"

"I don't know. The letter was here, on the counter when I came out of the kitchen. Is it bad news?"

"You could say that."

"Is there anything I can do to help?"

"I only wish there were."

Melissa knew she was, unwillingly, playing a game of cat and mouse with her unknown enemy. It was obvious the game was soon to be brought to a close. One way or the other.

The only way to guarantee her safety was to figure out who was behind Judith's attempted murder. As the police were getting nowhere fast, she must concentrate on solving the mystery herself. She was certain the same person was responsible for the threats on her own life.

The most logical place to start appeared to be the mansion. She must search the area for clues the police may have overlooked. Once she found the means by which the poison was administered, perhaps it would lead her to the person responsible.

Melissa phoned the mansion. Katherine answered. "Katherine, you are working late this evening?" Melissa denoted her surprise at hearing the estate manager's voice.

"Yes, I am a bit behind on a couple of things and thought I would catch up tonight. I am planning on going away for the weekend and needed to settle these matters before I left. What can I do for you, Mel?"

"I seem to have misplaced a favorite blouse of mine. It goes perfectly with my tweed suit and I am lost without it. The only place I can think of to look is in the guest room I occupied during my visit there. Would it be all right for me to come over in the morning and look for it?"

"No problem. I will tell Carmelita to expect you. Say about nine?"

"That will be fine. Running into Suzanne is something I prefer to avoid, if at all possible."

"I gathered as much. Can't say as I blame you."

"Pardon me for being nosy, Katherine, but I am surprised you are still working there. Considering all the disagreements you have had with Suzanne, I assumed, with Judith gone, she would dismiss you."

"She intended to, but we had a little chat. The estate would not run as smoothly without me and it would take a fair length of time to train a new person. Although she detests me, she detests work even more. She wisely chose to see things my way."

"I see. Well, I'm glad for you. It must be difficult, raising Cody by yourself."

"At times. But, I wouldn't have missed it for the world. We do all right, Cody and me. He is a fine boy."

"Most of which you can take credit for."

"Thank you, Melissa. That is kind of you to say."

The ladies said their goodbyes. Melissa was confused. Knowing Suzanne and her hatred for Katherine, she found it hard to believe that her cousin could be persuaded to keep the woman on. Perhaps it was as Katherine explained, Suzanne didn't relish the idea of additional work for herself. That being the case, why didn't she simply keep Katherine around until a suitable replacement could be trained? No, something did not add up. Oh well, one mystery to solve at a time.

Carmelita greeted her arrival the next morning, pleasantly, "Katherine told me you would be coming by. I was sorry Ms. Carson forced you to leave. I don't see how she can blame you for her mother's decision. Suzanne would have been unable to manage the agency. Everybody says so."

"Thanks, Carmelita. Sorry to intrude. It is just that I planned to wear my suit to work tomorrow and noticed the blouse was missing. It is not a problem if I look in the guest room for it?"

"Not at all." The woman added as an afterthought, "Why don't you check Suzanne's closet as well? I may have put it there by mistake, assuming it was hers."

"Should you go with me? In case Suzanne wonders who was in her room."

"That won't be necessary. I am in there all the time cleaning. Just be sure to put things back as you found them. Besides, Mother expects me to help make pies. If I don't get to it, she will think I am trying to weasel out of the job."

"Fine. Thanks."

After insuring her movements were unobserved, Melissa proceeded to Judith's room. The police seal had been removed and the door was unlocked. Despite a meticulous search, Melissa found nothing which could be helpful. The police had been thorough in their exploration, removing everything of significance.

Although she felt it was pointless, Melissa went to Suzanne's room. If Carmelita should join her to see if her search for the blouse was successful, it would be wise to appear to be looking for it. The maid was sure to find it odd, for her to have come all this way trying to retrieve the garment and stop before she had exhausted all possibilities.

It would take a while to survey Suzanne's extensive wardrobe. Time she did not have. Melissa intended on making a cursory check only, merely to avoid raising suspicion.

As she drew her fictitious search to a close, Melissa spied a small jewelry box, partially concealed amid the vast array of hand-crafted sweaters piled neatly on shelves, occupying a section to the right interior of the closet.

What a strange place to store a jewelry box, Mel thought, knowing Suzanne kept her more valuable accessories in the library wall safe. Curiosity overcame her inclination to respect her cousin's right to privacy. She carefully opened the box. Its contents did not, even faintly, resemble jewelry.

Melissa desperately tried to fathom why Suzanne would have, in her possession, a glass hypodermic syringe, with an assortment of disposable needle tips. If the items were necessary for treatment of a medical problem, such as diabetes, why were they hidden? Diabetics, Melissa knew, must use syringes calibrated in units, due to the precision needed for the small amount administered. These came equipped with their own individual needle, both needle and syringe disposed of after each use. No, Suzanne must have had another use for the equipment. Mel was puzzled as to why the woman had not discarded the needle, now that the purpose for which they had been used was accomplished. Perhaps she intended to, once she could do so secretly. With so many people around the estate, chances are, unless she picked the perfect time, it would be difficult to avoid having her activity observed.

Cautiously wrapping the box in tissue paper and placing it in her pocket, she started to make her exit. A voice behind her startled the woman. "Melissa, did you find what you were looking for?" the voice asked.

Melissa took a couple of deep breaths to slow her heartbeat, before turning to face Carmelita. "Pardon me?" she said, afraid the maid had seen her remove the box from Suzanne's closet.

"Your blouse. Did you find it?"

"No. I must have forgotten to bring it with me." But, I found something much more interesting, Mel thought to herself.

"That's a shame. I will keep on the lookout for it and call you if it turns up."

"Thanks, Carmelita. Well, I had better get to the office. See you later."

Melissa had no intention of going to the office just yet. She had more important business to conduct with Detective Rawlins.

The woman who entered Suzanne's room following Mel's departure was pleased to see the bait had been accepted. Awfully decent for Mel to phone and announce her planned visit to the mansion. It would seem logical to search Suzanne's room for a misplaced blouse. Where else would it be found? She had been in a quandary as to how to implicate Judith's daughter in the woman's murder. Mel had solved the problem for her. Once the police tested the syringe and found it contained arsenic they would have no choice but to arrest Suzanne. God, she hated that woman. Who better to frame for the murder? A shame the remainder of her problems could not be solved as easily.

25

Melissa wasted little time getting to the police station. Perhaps this new evidence would be the catalyst she had been searching for to make Suzanne talk.

Due to the complexity of the attempt made on Judith's life and the embezzlement scheme, Melissa knew her cousin was not the master mind behind these events. No doubt the man who had interfered with her brakes and tried to drive her off the road could lay claim to that title.

Immediately upon arriving at the station, Mel was granted an audience with the detective. "You have some news for me, Miss?" he greeted.

"Yes, sir." Melissa took the box from her pocket, opening it to reveal the contents within.

"What do we have here?" The man was suitably impressed.

"I found this in Suzanne Carson's closet. Undoubtedly, the syringe will show traces of arsenic."

"We will have it tested immediately. Looks as though you have answered one of my questions."

"Which question was that?" asked Mel.

"How the arsenic got into Mrs. Carson's vitamin capsules. The lab technician said it would have to be injected. He noticed a small pin hole on the capsule end. The vitamin liquid was withdrawn and replaced with a solution containing the poison."

"God!" exclaimed Mel, "I forgot all about Judith's vitamins. But that would not account for the dose which killed her."

"Oh that. We think it was added to her glass of warm milk and the glass was removed before we got a chance to check it. Someone must have replaced it with a clean one. If we can find out who was giving her the regular dose, we can assume they were also responsible for administering the lethal one. If this syringe shows traces of arsenic that will solve the mystery of who put the poison in the capsules? It seems I am making progress on all counts today."

"Really."

"Yes. We found Ms. Carson's fingerprints on the tire iron that was used to kill Mr. Dunn. That lady has a pile of explaining to do."

"There is one thing we may be overlooking."

"Yes."

"What if the evidence against Suzanne was placed there by someone wishing to frame her. As we both know, she is not well liked. Is it possible that the real criminal is using that fact to their advantage? It is hardly a secret that she had excellent motives for both murders."

"There you go, defending her again. I don't understand you."

"I know," said Mel, acknowledging her illogical conduct. "It is just that I would hate to see anyone convicted of a crime they did not commit, just because no one liked them."

"Even Suzanne."

"Yes, even Suzanne."

"Ms. Sommers, I cannot ignore the facts. All the evidence points to your cousin. Unlike yourself, I cannot allow emotions to sway my thinking. I have to act on what information I have."

"That goes without saying. But, that doesn't mean you have to close your mind to the possibility of a frame-up."

"Ms. Sommers, I never close my mind to any new developments." The detective was agitated by Melissa's implication that he would not be receptive to facts proving Suzanne's innocence. "If you can bring me proof to support your theory I will be all ears, believe me. For now, I have a job to do and I plan to do it. Excuse me."

Detective Rawlins abruptly brought their conversation to a close.

Melissa was as perplexed over her own actions as the detective was. She had found the needle in Suzanne's closet. The woman had a strong motive for both murders. Mel was convinced her cousin was withholding information about something. There was just one problem: she did not honestly believe Suzanne could murder anyone. If for no other reason than that it would be too much work. Hire the job out: yes. Perform the act herself: no.

Mel could not picture her cousin standing behind a man and bashing in his skull with a tire iron. Just as she could not envision her carefully withdrawing liquid from a capsule, then replacing it with poison. Much too tenuous.

But, her prints were found on the tire iron. Knowing Suzanne, it was highly unlikely they would get there from her employment of the tool for the purpose for which it was intended.

Just one second, Melissa thought. Considering where they found Mark's body, his assailant had to be someone the young man felt comfortable enough with to invite into his apartment. Someone he felt safe turning his back on. Suzanne would hardly fit the bill.

And the man who had threatened Melissa. Where did he fit into the picture?

Fleeting images kept invading her mind. Images of the man in the restaurant. A man she had seen somewhere before. But where? If only she could remember.

She set out for the agency to tell Timothy about the new evidence she had uncovered and what Detective Rawlins had revealed. She regretted being unable to advise him of her conversation with Raymond. Unfortunately, that was impossible. To do so would involve telling him Judith was alive. Such knowledge could not be divulged. Not without the consent of the others.

When she arrived at her office, her secretary announced the presence of a young man who wished to speak with her. Instructing the woman to bid him entrance, she awaited him in her office.

"You don't know me Ms. Sommers," the man began. "My name is Adam Ilsley. I work in the messenger department. Mark Dunn was a good friend of mine. Indirectly, that is what convinced me to come to see you. At first I hesitated, not sure how you would respond to what I had to say." Adam paused at this juncture, as if needing encouragement to continue. Encouragement he promptly received.

"Please go on, Mr. Ilsley," said Mel.

"It involves Ms. Carson."

"Yes."

"You see, Ms. Carson has been having a relationship, if you know what I mean, with Paul Lakefield. He works in the creative department as an artist. Mark learned about their affair and told me. We laughed about it, thinking that it hardly fit Ms. Carson's image, to be involved with an employee.

"When Ms. Carson arranged to have Mark fired, we figured she had found out that he knew about her and Paul. She dismissed him before he could spread the word around. That was why I didn't tell anyone sooner. I was scared she would get rid of me too.

"Anyway, a couple of days ago, I saw Paul go into the

accounting department, after the others had gone home. He didn't see me. I wondered what he was doing in there and how he got in. Then I saw it. He had a key.

"Don't you see? He is the embezzler. Probably working with Ms. Carson. They were afraid Mark knew about their scheme, so they killed him. They killed Mark, Ms. Sommers. As sure as I am sitting here, they killed him. I should have come to you sooner with what I knew, but I was scared. I can't afford to lose my job."

"Your hesitation is understandable, Adam. Especially in view of what happened to your friend. I am glad you came to me now. We will look into what you have told me."

The young man left, relieved after clearing his conscience. His exit was immediately followed by Timothy's entrance. "I've got it. I know who the embezzler is," he said, waving a piece of paper enthusiastically.

"Really, so do I," announced Mel.

"It has to be Paul Lakefield."

"Yes, but how did you figure it out?"

"His signature. It has the artistic flair Mrs. Newton spoke of. There is also the fact that he is an artist by trade."

"And," Mel interjected, "he is having an affair with Suzanne, which is probably how he got a key to the accounting department."

"How do you know that?"

"That man that was just here."

"Yes, I know him, Adam Ilsley. He works with our messenger service."

"He told me Mark knew of their relationship. Adam believes Mark was fired because they were afraid he suspected what they were really up to, in regard to the embezzlement scheme."

"Did Mark give any indication to Adam that he suspected such to be the case?"

"No. I don't know if he really suspected anything. It seems as though it was more fear on the part of Paul and Suzanne, that he may have known more than he admitted."

"So, what do we do now?"

"Oh my God!" Mel exclaimed, looking at the paper Timothy handed to her.

"What is wrong?" asked Timothy.

"That's him. That's the man."

"What man? Melissa, what are you talking about?"

Melissa realized she had to tell Timothy where she saw Paul Lakefield. "The other evening I had dinner with a friend of mine. I sensed someone was following me. When we left the restaurant, he was sitting at a booth. I knew I had seen him somewhere before but could not, for the life of me, remember where.

"On my way home a car came up behind me and bumped me."

"Was he trying to force you off the road?"

"I don't think so. The bump wasn't forceful enough for me to completely lose control of the car. I got the feeling it was just a warning. There was a note waiting for me when I got to the inn." Melissa showed the memo to Timothy. "Obviously, he was the one who tampered with my brakes."

"So what do we do now?" asked Tim.

"We inform Detective Rawlins of our findings. He has some things to discuss with Suzanne anyway. This will just add to the list." Melissa proceeded to fill the assistant manager in on what she knew.

"And what of Paul?"

"We'll leave him to Rawlins as well. The man is dangerous. I don't think we should face him alone."

Mel was unable to contact Detective Rawlins, the officer answering the phone informing her that he had left for the day. Mel knew where he had gone. No doubt he was headed for the Carson estate. She would try to reach him there.

26

Constance Carson's return home was unheralded. The children had been returned to boarding school and she to her boring, albeit wealthy, existence.

She reflected on how empty her life had become and found herself surprisingly unable to rationalize her feelings of dissatisfaction. Fundamentally, her routine was unchanged.

Perhaps that is the problem, she thought. I need some variety to provide stimulation.

Judith was gone now. Thank God. Now Donald would see some real money.

She had not returned for her mother-in-law's funeral. Connie was many things but she was not a hypocrite. She had never been fond of Donald's mother. A feeling which had been mutual.

Knowing the vast wealth her husband would now have at his disposal should have and did, though only fleetingly, make her delirious with gratitude. After all, wasn't that what she had done all this for. The money. It was a startling revelation to discover that now the day of unlimited resources had arrived, she remained unfulfilled.

Donald had warned her about Melissa inheriting the agency but Connie knew they could contest the will and probably win. She refused to believe anything else. Not after all she had been through with this family.

Maybe I should suggest to Donald that we go away. Take a trip. Just the two of us. Connie was diligently attempting to think of ways to rejuvenate her mundane existence. Perhaps a trip could rekindle the magic that had once existed in her marriage. Magic that had been absent for years.

Connie could not remember when she had last made love to her husband. Nor could she recall any occasion, as of late, when she had had to repel his advances. He must have taken the hint and accepted her rejection. He had stopped trying. Finally getting the message that she was simply not interested.

What she had failed to accept, when marrying Donald, was that mere riches cannot make a relationship work. She thought, at the time, that she could learn to endure living with a man she did not love. If there was enough money to compensate. She had been wrong, desperately wrong.

What was even more frightening was the possibility that her husband no longer loved her. A development she had never before considered and one that, if true, altered the course of things. As long as his feelings were still strong, she was in the driver's seat. Or so she thought. She could always twirl him around her little finger. He could refuse her nothing. Now, all that could be changed.

He had tolerated her endless affairs for the sake of the children and because of his intense adoration for her. Lately he seemed totally unaware of her late nights out and, though prepared with an excuse, she was not required to give one. Stepping out on one's husband was hardly as exciting if he did not care. The anger he had once displayed upon learning of her latest conquest had been replaced with ambivalence. She preferred the anger. At least it was a reaction. A negative response, but at least it was something.

Only a woman as self-absorbed as Connie Carson would fail to contemplate the probability that her husband, whose advances she had spurned, could find comfort and a receptive port for those advances elsewhere. It had not, for one moment, crossed her mind that Donald would have any desire to look for sexual fulfillment with someone other than his wife. Once again, she was wrong.

Donald was a very attractive man. A fact which, while escaping his wife's awareness, was not lost on other women of his acquaintance. Women who did not find his monetary wealth an issue in their degree of receptiveness.

Such a woman was Meredith Walker, the newest addition to the agency's accounting department. Connie would be surprised to learn that, as she was traveling in a cab toward the estate, her husband was deep in conversation with that particular young lady.

"When is your wife arriving home?" asked Meredith.

"I'm not certain but I believe it is today. The boys are due back in school tomorrow," answered Donald.

"Why did you send your children to a boarding school? Wouldn't you rather have them with you?"

"That was Connie's decision. She never has found any pleasure in motherhood. It tends to interfere with her other activities.

All of her friends place their children in boarding schools. They suggested Connie do the same, so she did."

"Shouldn't you have had some say in that decision?"

"I tried to convince Connie to allow them to remain at home. She would not hear of it. As she said, I am at the office all day and often am gone for days at a time on business trips. She is the one they would spend most of their time with."

"You could have hired a nanny," suggested Meredith.

"We did, when the boys were small. Even then, they

preferred to be with their mother. Connie didn't mind it, she loves babies. Babies are cute. She enjoyed showing them off to her friends. Changing and feeding them were chores she was not required to do: the nanny took care of those unpleasant duties. Connie was like a little girl with a doll. It was only when they advanced to the child phase that they become intolerable for her."

"That is so sad. How often do you get to see them?"

"Holidays and two weeks in August. The rest of the summer they are enrolled in camp. They are nice boys and they love their mother dearly. Fortunately, they have no idea she cannot bear to have them around for any length of time."

"So what happens to us, now that your wife is returning?" Meredith was afraid to hear the answer to her question.

"I plan to tell Connie I want a divorce. Immediately."

"Please don't say that just to make me feel better."

"I'm not. It is what I want. What I have wanted for a long time. Just never had the nerve to suggest it, before I met you."

The lady talking with him, though shy in the midst of a crowd, showed no evidence of it in the company of one. Against her own better judgment and that of her friends Meredith had entered into the affair with Donald Carson, with both eyes open.

She knew statistics showed that married men rarely left their wives for their lovers. She admitted she was taking a serious risk of being hurt. But, for her, it was worth it. The time she spent with him was worth the time she elected to spend alone. He evoked emotions in her she had never before experienced. Meredith loved this man deeply and would settle for what he offered. How long she would be satisfied, sharing him with his wife and family, she could not say and he did not ask. They had seldom discussed his marital situation. When they did, the topic was initiated by Donald.

For now, she was content with things as they were. She enjoyed her work and those she worked with. She had this wonderful man as a part of her life. That was enough. Much more than what most people had.

Donald, inexperienced in women's ways, was surprised at Meredith's failure to pressure him into procuring a divorce. He had never been involved in an extramarital relationship prior to his present arrangement. He had overheard conversations between men who made running around on their wives an art form. A vocation they seemed more dedicated to, and definitely put more energy into, than they did their careers. To tell the truth the same could be said of his wife. A person certainly had to have a vivid imagination to think up so many lies as to how they spent their time.

In every instance he was familiar with, the mistress (what an ugly, archaic term) usually made constant demands on the man to leave his wife. Donald gathered it was this ever-increasing pressure on the man to leave his family and the man's failure to do so, that ultimately ended the affair. Most men had no intention of changing their marital status when they began the extramarital liaison. They only used the promise to do so as a bargaining tool, to keep the woman hanging on.

Donald was not like most men. He felt it was unfair to lead Meredith on with a promise he had no intention of fulfilling. He did not think of Meredith as his possession or "mistress." Rather as the most important person in his life.

Donald had no wish to continue pursuing a mutually unsatisfying marriage with Connie. He wanted out and he was going to get out. No matter the cost. When his divorce was final he planned to marry Meredith, if she would have him.

"Donald are you sure now is the right time, with your Mother's death and everything going on with the agency? Won't that be more traumatic for your children?

"You don't have to do this for me, you know. It is not that I will be overjoyed to know you are leaving me to go home to her, but when you decide to ask her for a divorce, it should be for the right reasons. Not because you feel any pressure from me."

"Meredith, I have never left you to go home to her, as you put it. Connie and I have not slept together since I met you. On that you have my word.

"I am asking my wife for a divorce, because that is what I want. I want to be with you and only you. Do you understand? More importantly, is that what you want?"

"Yes, to both questions. I want that more than anything in the world."

"Fine. That is all I need to know."

"I better get back to work. People will wonder where I am."

"I will call you later. If Connie arrives home tonight, it is as good a time as any to speak with her about the divorce."

Meredith left Donald to his thoughts. Pleasant thoughts, mingled with ones of pain. Pleasure when thinking of the life that lay ahead: a life with Meredith. Pain for what he would be leaving behind. Mistakes he had made. The most obvious one being his choice of spousal partner.

He felt guilty for the children. While being the product of a broken home no longer held the stigma it once did (in some circles it was almost a status symbol), the fact that his sons were to become one of that group was regrettable. Unavoidable, but regrettable all the same. Their parents' divorce was certain to disrupt the security and continuity in their young lives. On the other hand, to stay together just for the children's sake, seldom was successful. Children could see through the facade. His sons had suggested as much during their recent stint at home.

Home, what a powerful word. There were so many connotations attached to it. He remembered a statement his mother had made when he was just a lad. "A house is the building you live in. A home is the love you find there." If that were true, Donald's house had not been a home for some time.

He planned to change all that. One thing he had with Meredith was love. If he lost most of his wealth in exchange for the future this lovely lady offered him, so be it. It was worth losing it all.

27

Donald's arrival at the estate coincided with his wife's departure. She had planned an engagement for the evening and, after refreshing herself upon her return home, was ready to set out for her date. Donald, however, had other plans. "Connie," he said, not bothering to welcome her home, "we have to talk."

"Fine. We can discuss whatever it is when I get back," his wife replied, her manner nonchalant.

"No, it can't wait. We will talk now." Donald's voice held an authoritative air Connie had not previously been exposed to, one she felt it was wise not to ignore.

"Donald, I have made plans for the evening. Can't it wait?"

"Connie, your rendezvous will have to take place some other time. I suggest you call your friend and advise him of your inability to keep your appointment. Join me, in the study, in five minutes."

"If you insist," she said, making no reference to his insinuating comment. There was little sense in denying an accusation which they both knew was factual. She took the time to call the man she was scheduled to meet, before proceeding to the study.

"Okay Donald," she began. "What is so all fired urgent that couldn't wait for a couple of hours?"

"Connie, I want a divorce. I want it now. I strongly recommend you do not oppose it. Unless, of course, you have no objection to airing your dirty laundry in public." Donald amazed himself at the bluntness of his opening comment.

"Donald!" his wife exclaimed. "What are you talking about?"

"That should be obvious, my dear, even to you. I am tired. Tired of this sham of a marriage we are involved in. Tired of the constant bickering. Tired of your endless affairs and attempts to embarrass me. Tired of the ever present put downs and sarcastic remarks about my manhood. But, most of all, Connie, I am tired of you."

"My, aren't we being dramatic. You must be taking lessons from your sister. This seems an odd time to be talking of divorce. When we finally have everything we've ever wanted."

"Don't you mean when you have everything you've ever wanted? Enough money for you to treat yourself the way you feel you deserve to be treated. The prestige and social status that comes with being a Carson. Freedom to come and go whenever, and with whomever, you please. Life couldn't be better for you, could it? Well, I want more and I plan to have it."

"If this is about my extracurricular activities, I will curtail the frequency with which I go out. I was thinking, on my way home, we should take a trip. A second honeymoon. Perhaps we could rekindle what we once had."

"A second honeymoon is not the answer. Connie, face it, you don't love me. I doubt if you ever did. And I, most definitely, no longer love you.

"Let's be frank, shall we. You married me for my money. I know that and you know that. I was misguided into believing you genuinely cared for me. That was a mistake. I see that now, in fact I have for a long time."

"But…" stammered Connie. This was not going well at all. She had assumed Donald would want her forever. The only way she contemplated their marriage ending in divorce was if she instigated it. Sure, she would receive a large settlement. Her lawyer would see to that. But, what of the social position Donald had alluded to. She enjoyed being a Carson, living in a fine mansion, with the respect afforded her, due to the family connections. She would lose all of that if Donald divorced her.

In desperation, Connie resorted to using the only ammunition she had remaining. The children. "You'll never see your boys. I will make sure of that. If you divorce me, you divorce them."

"I hardly think so, Connie. Not only will I see them, I plan to petition for custody of them."

"The courts will never award you custody. I am their mother. Mothers always get custody."

"Not necessarily. Considering your conduct, you hardly qualify as a fit mother. I have people who will testify to your indiscretions, should that become necessary." As several of Connie's liaisons were with close friends of her husband, she knew his claim to be true. The ones she had dumped would like nothing better than to have the opportunity to get back at her.

"I don't understand, Donald. Nothing has changed in our relationship. You seemed to accept the way things were."

"There are two things which persuaded me to make this change now. One is your callused reaction to Mother's death. God, Connie, you never even came to her funeral.

"Secondly, I have met someone else. A woman who I love dearly and who, unselfishly, loves me. She loves me," he repeated forcefully, "not my money, but me, for the person I am."

"I see. Some little tart has been warming your bed. Really Donald, a casual affair hardly constitutes reason for divorce. I don't mind if you have your fun. Actually, it is a relief. It spares me the effort of having to think up excuses not to welcome your advances myself. It could make our marriage better. We could arrive at an understanding, suiting both of our needs."

Donald could not believe the callousness of the woman he had once loved. "Connie, the relationship I am involved in is more than a casual affair. Unlike your endless string of sexual partners, I truly love the lady. As for expecting sexual favors from you, that has ceased to be an issue for some time now."

"So, you have decided to forfeit what we have for the sake of some little tramp."

"Connie, I have never laid a finger on you with violent intentions. If you wish that trend to continue, you would be well-advised to curtail any derogatory reference you consider making against a woman who is more of a lady than you will ever be."

The facial slap that was Connie's response to his remark, while unwise, was inevitable. So predictable, in fact, that Donald succeeded in blocking her hand before it reached its intended target. As Donald firmly held her arm, Connie burst into tears. "Donald," she accused, "how can you do this to me? The humiliation of a divorce will make it impossible for me to be seen in public."

"Don't be ridiculous, Connie. Three-quarters of the ladies you associate with have been divorced two or three times. I hardly think they will be shocked by yours. If you find the idea of our divorce so humiliating, perhaps it would have been wise to consider the possibility before you started looking in other areas for what you had at home. You have only yourself to blame."

"You will pay and pay dearly for this decision, Donald."

"Of that I have no doubt. Just remember, money has never

meant as much to me as it has to you, or my sister. You can have the money, if the courts allocate it to you. I simply want my freedom and, no matter what you do, that I will have.

"I have spoken with Raymond, instructing him to begin divorce proceedings. So you see, this is not a whim on my part. Your lawyer will be receiving the papers any day now. I thought you should be prepared."

Connie was devastated. Under no circumstances had she envisioned this turn of events. She was, mistakenly, under the impression her marriage was under control. Though, arguably not a conventional arrangement, it appeared workable. At least, until recently.

She had sensed Donald's changing attitude toward her, but had interpreted it as a temporary dissatisfaction. A mid-life crisis, so to speak. She knew this happened to men, from time to time. Thus, her suggestion of the second honeymoon. A proposal, she now realized, had been delayed too long. Had she possessed the foresight to arrange a trip for herself and her husband months ago, Connie was certain of her ability to have persuaded him to remain in the marriage.

Connie was a beautiful woman. The type of female from whom models are created. She knew how to use her body to please a man.

Her only misfortune had been in choosing to use her sexual prowess for the satisfaction of men other than her husband.

Donald was not a man to be content with simply having a fine-looking woman on his arm. Connie had misjudged his complacency of late as acceptance of their marital situation, rather than considering the possibility of him having found someone else. Her error in judgment would cost her dearly.

28

The divorce discussion was not the only unpleasantness to befall the Carson household that evening. As planned, Detective Rawlins was making an unannounced visit to the estate. Equipped with the information obtained from lab tests carried out on the syringe Mel had discovered, Mike was prepared to arrest Suzanne Carson for the murders of her mother and Mark Dunn.

Mike sensed the tension in the air when he entered the mansion. As no one knew of his intended visit, the atmosphere could not be attributed to his arrival. The most hostile vibrations were bouncing between Donald Carson and a stunning blonde whom Rawlins assumed was his wife. This hypothesis was soon confirmed through introductions.

Mike was perplexed over the animosity radiating between the couple, especially upon being informed that Donald's wife had just returned from a two week stint with relatives. Most couples, having spent time apart, resent any intrusion on their privacy. Wishing to make up for the time they had lost. Such was not the case with this pair. On the contrary, they seemed to welcome the interruption.

"I am here to inform you that we have, in our possession, evidence leading us to the identity of the person responsible for murdering Mrs. Carson and Mark Dunn."

"Really, Detective. That is excellent. So you were able to retrieve prints from the rat poison can?" Donald, relieved that this business would soon be over, wished to learn how the information was obtained.

"No, it had been wiped clean of prints. However, we know the arsenic was injected into the woman's vitamin pills. We have, in our possession, the needle which was used to accomplish the task. This, combined with the prints we found on the tire iron, is sufficient evidence to make an arrest."

"Great. When will you be apprehending the culprit?" asked Donald.

"Right now, sir," announced the detective. Turning to Suzanne, the policeman directed his next comment toward the woman. "Ms. Carson, I am here to advise you of your rights and arrest you for the murder of your mother and Mark Dunn." After the initial gasp escaped from her mouth, Suzanne was speechless, a condition advantageous to the reading of her rights.

Following that procedure, Rawlins asked the stunned woman, "Do you understand your rights, as I have read them to you?"

"Yes," she said, in a voice barely above a whisper.

Prepared to hear her usual outburst, the assembled group was astonished that it was not forthcoming. She simply said, "I did not do this."

"I'm sorry, Miss," the detective said, "but the evidence says you did. I have no choice but to take you in."

"Call Raymond, Donald." The woman instructed her brother. "It will kill me to have to be in jail. See what he can do?"

"I will, Sis, don't worry."

After answering a few more questions from Donald, Detective Rawlins escorted the woman to the waiting police car which would take her to the local jail, where she would be held until her preliminary court hearing.

Donald was more disturbed by his sister's reaction to her incarceration, than by the actual arrest itself. She appeared to have lost her fighting spirit. There was no doubt in his mind that she did not commit these murders, but why did she not display more resistance to the detective's accusations. It was unlike Suzanne to be so calm.

His sister had been framed. Of that, Donald was certain. The question was, how was he to prove it.

Despite his belief in his sister, Donald knew that her inability to get along well with others would make it almost impossible to find individuals who would be supportive. It would be equally difficult to get any assistance in trying to prove her innocence. Suzanne had burned her share of bridges, in arriving at her present station in life. She had inflicted damage to past friendships. Irreparable damage.

Considering the way she had been treating Raymond of late, it was possible the lawyer would not consent to take her case. Without him, she was out in the cold as far as legal counsel was concerned. Donald hardly considered the poor excuse for a lawyer Suzanne had recently consulted (in regard to contesting the will), adequate legal representation. Even if Donald had held a higher opinion of the man, it was unlikely an attorney who specialized in civil law would be of much assistance in a criminal case. No, Raymond was their best hope.

Raymond listened, intently, as Donald explained the predicament facing Suzanne. "They seem to have a strong case against her, Donald." Although he did not want to admit it, Donald knew this to be true. The detective had established motive, means, and opportunity. Hard evidence to crack.

"One thing does seem a bit odd."

"What is that?" asked Donald, anxious for even the slightest glimmer of hope.

"It is strange that they found Suzanne's fingerprints on the tire iron, when they were unable to retrieve any from the equipment used to kill your mother. How did they account for that?"

"I asked Detective Rawlins that very question. He feels Suzanne, suspecting Mel and Timothy were planning to meet with the man, was rushed when she killed Mark, thus not having adequate time to wipe the prints off the tire iron. He does not believe she initially planned to kill him. Rawlins thinks she took the tire iron with her as protection, in case the young man became violent. Perhaps she tried to reason with him and he would not oblige. So, in a fit of rage, she killed him."

"Sounds plausible."

"I don't buy it," said Donald. "Ray, can you honestly tell me that you can picture my sister bashing in some fellow's skull?"

"I didn't say I believe that is what happened. But, they have a theory which the district attorney would say bears consideration. Unless we can prove otherwise, Suzanne will, most likely, be convicted."

"I know she has treated you abominably, Ray, but I don't know where else to turn. Will you help me?"

"Of course, Donald. I will do what I can."

Raymond was compelled to agree with Donald that the only way to guarantee Suzanne's freedom was to solve the mystery themselves. He had the option of revealing his knowledge of Judith's continued existence. However, that would only reduce the charge to attempted murder of Mrs. Carson, which carried a similar penalty. And there would still be the allegation of Mark's murder to deal with.

When Donald hung up from his phone conversation with Raymond, Melissa called, asking to speak with Detective

Rawlins. Donald provided the details of Suzanne's arrest to his cousin.

"I'm sorry, Donald. Truly I am. If Suzanne is, indeed, innocent I'm sure the truth will come out."

"I hope so, Mel."

After speaking with Donald, Melissa called the jail, with the hope of reaching the detective before he left that establishment. She was in luck.

"Yes, Ms. Sommers," said Mike, when he came on the line.

Melissa gave the policeman what information they had on Paul Lakefield, including his current address.

"Sounds as though I should pay a visit to Lakefield's residence. Maybe I have the wrong person locked up, after all."

"It is a possibility he killed Mark. However, he would not have had access to Judith. Someone else had to help him poison her."

"That someone else being her daughter," suggested Mike.

"Possibly. I cannot figure out why she would keep the evidence lying around, though. Why wouldn't she have disposed of the syringe, the same time she discarded the rat poison bottle?"

"Perhaps she thought it might come in handy again. In case someone else got in her way. Or, she may have simply not had a chance to dispose of it safely."

"I suppose."

"I will let you know when we apprehend Mr. Lakefield. Thank you, Ms. Sommers for your assistance."

"One other thing, Detective."

"Yes," prompted Mike.

"Suzanne was unaware of our meeting with Mark. Sure, she knew we were looking into the circumstances behind his dismissal, but we didn't tell her about the meeting."

"Even if that is true, it makes little difference. She probably realized you would be speaking with the young man as soon as possible. That being the case, either her or Lakefield decided to get there first."

"Yes, but, as I understand it, you believe the reason Suzanne's fingerprints were found on the tire iron was because she was in a rush. If she was unaware of our scheduled meeting with Mark, what would create the rush?"

"Anything. After all, the man was murdered in his own apartment. Perhaps whoever killed him heard someone coming. Or, if she hadn't intended on killing him, the very fact that she did may have scared her enough to make her forget about wiping the prints from the weapon.

"In the case of Mrs. Carson's murder, I believe we have a premeditated crime. I'm not certain that is true of Mr. Dunn's. Regardless of the definition, however, murder is murder. Premeditated, or not, it still stinks."

"Well," said Mel, speaking with Timothy, after her chat with the detective. "We have done all we can do. The rest is up to Mike."

29

The next morning Melissa and Timothy accompanied Raymond to the jail to visit Suzanne. She was taken from her holding cell to the visitors' room when they arrived. Having heard no news from Detective Rawlins, they assumed Paul Lakefield was still free. The trio hoped Suzanne could give them some basis with which to prove her innocence. If, indeed, that was the case. Despite the substantial evidence Detective Rawlins had gathered supporting the case against Suzanne, Melissa was of the belief that the mystery was a far cry from being solved.

She was stunned by the woman's appearance. Suzanne looked haggard and unkempt and had obviously been crying. Altogether, presenting the image of a broken woman.

"I am glad to see you," she said. "Are you here to take me home?"

"Not just yet, Suzanne," stated Mel, wishing she could fulfill the woman's plea. "We have to ask you some questions. Questions which may help us discover who framed you. You must understand how important it is that you are totally honest with your answers."

"Ask away, I have no fight left in me."

"We know about you and Paul Lakefield. Were you aware he was the one embezzling the money from the agency?" Mel, as was her nature, came straight to the point.

"I knew he was responsible for the falsified orders. Mother was not the one who spoke to him about it. I did. I warned him that, if Mother were to find out what he was doing, she was sure to fire him. So, he stopped, before she found him out. I wasn't certain he was behind this recent scheme, though I had my suspicions he was involved."

"Did you give him a key to the accounting department?"

"No, though he was in a position, on more than one occasion, to remove it from my purse and have it copied. I imagine that is precisely what he did."

"Why didn't you tell us if you suspected him?" demanded Timothy. "Or reveal your knowledge of the part he played in the previous case?"

"I couldn't. I knew, if I told you, you would learn of our relationship and assume I was involved in his plan. Besides, I had no proof."

"And what of Mark Dunn. Did you know he killed Mark Dunn?"

Raymond was tempted, for the first time in his life, to strike a woman. Not being a violent man, he berated himself for allowing such primal instincts to enter his thoughts. As it was, he settled for shaking her, more forcefully than was perhaps necessary, but certainly not enough to do her any physical harm. It was difficult to say who was more startled by the action, Suzanne or Raymond.

"Yes, I knew!" she exclaimed. "I didn't want to believe it,

but I was sure he was the one who murdered that nice young man!"

"Suzanne, how could you sit still and allow such a thing to take place, without trying to stop it?" accused Mel.

"Because she is selfish, that's why. Selfish and unfeeling," responded Raymond, visibly disturbed by what the woman had revealed.

"Raymond, you don't have to be so harsh," said Mel, realizing her cousin evidently regretted her decision to remain quiet. No doubt wishing she had done something to prevent the murder of Mark Dunn.

"No, he's right. I am selfish. Mother tried to tell me so, but I wouldn't listen. The only thing I cared about was myself and how the knowledge of Paul's activities would reflect upon me.

"Paul wanted me to fire Mark because he knew about our relationship. At least, that was the excuse he used for wanting him out of the way. I realize, now, that was a smoke screen. He was afraid Mark knew about his illegal activities.

"God, I barely knew Mark Dunn. I only met him a few times when he delivered my mail. He did bring it to me directly, on the rare occasion when my secretary was out of the office. He was so polite and mannerly. Even called me Ma'am, not Ms. Carson like everyone else." At this juncture Suzanne began to cry. "God, I can't believe I allowed Paul to convince me to fire him. How could I have been so cruel?"

"Not much wonder Mark was confused as to why he was released," commented Timothy.

"I told Paul you were looking into Mark's dismissal. He said he would 'handle Mark'. I wondered what he meant, but I didn't really want to know.

"When you told me the young man was dead I was relieved. I can't believe it. I was relieved!" she repeated, for emphasis.

"Glad that he could not reveal what he knew about me. Can you believe that?"

The trio could, indeed, believe it. They were, however, noticeably impressed by the overnight transformation in the woman. Had they known this would be the result, they would have recommended placing her in a jail cell overnight sooner. Then again, maybe not. The change was definitely for the better, but it was sad to see the woman in such a state.

"Mark may have told him that he knew what he was up to, meaning your affair, but Paul interpreted it as meaning he knew about his participation in the embezzlement." All agreed that Timothy's hypothesis, as to Paul's reaction, was a valid one.

"How did your fingerprints get on the tire iron?" asked Mel.

"That was easy enough. It was my tire iron. Paul was with me one evening when the car had a flat. He changed it, but I passed him the tire iron and put it back in the trunk. Paul wore gloves, I didn't. He must have got it out of my car the day he killed Mark."

"Did you have anything to do with your mother's poisoning?" asked Raymond.

"No, I did not!" Suzanne said, emphatically. Some of her fire had returned. "Mother and I have not been close for many years, but I did love her, in my own way. I just had trouble expressing it."

"Do you think Paul was involved in her removal?" asked Timothy.

"No, how could he have been? I was the only person he knew at the mansion and he sure didn't get any help from me."

"Well," said Mel. "We will have to look elsewhere for Judith's killer."

"Just a second," announced a voice behind them. Everyone turned to face Donald, who had joined the group. "I just remembered something. Katherine, our estate manager, she was married to a Lakefield for a short time. He is Cody's father. She didn't tell me but a friend of mine recognized her and referred to her as Kathy Lakefield. Do you suppose Paul is her ex-husband? After all, Lakefield is hardly a common name."

"That could explain it. We don't get along very well, she and I," announced Suzanne.

"If you don't get along, why did you keep her on, when Judith passed away?" asked Mel.

"Because she knew about Paul and I and threatened to spread the word of our affair. I had no problem with her work. She is extremely competent. We agreed that we would stay out of each other's way and she would remain working for us, until she received her inheritance from Mother's will. Cody, her son, is a sweet boy. Although I dislike Katherine, I would hate to see him suffer."

"If Paul is her ex-husband that would explain how she learned about your relationship. Could she have helped him murder Judith?" suggested Melissa.

"Oh, I don't think so," answered Donald. "As much as she detests Suzanne, she loved Mother immensely. They had a rapport rarely seen between employer and secretary."

"What if he gave her little choice, maybe using the boy as incentive to persuade her cooperation?" continued Mel.

"That is the only way she would have done it. Cody is her whole life," stated Donald.

"Aren't we getting a bit carried away with suppositions here?" Raymond reminded the rest of their total lack of evidence to support this premise.

"You're right. We will have to talk with Katherine before we carry this any farther." Mel recognized the wisdom in Raymond's statement.

After the group left the jail, Donald remaining to visit with his sister, they planned their strategy.

"I still believe the information we seek is at the mansion," said Mel. "I will go there today and check it out. It is Carmelita and Anna's day off. They usually visit Anna's father at the nursing home this time of day. Connie will be shopping. That is all she ever does. Katherine will be alone. If I talk with her, perhaps we can clear up some of this mess."

"Do you think that is wise? We do not know, for a fact, that she was not cooperating with Lakefield. Don't you think it would be safer if I went along?" Timothy did not feel it prudent for Melissa to face the woman alone.

"I will not tell her we suspect her of helping Paul. We don't even know if the man is her ex. I plan to imply that we believe Suzanne is responsible, but we need more evidence to prove it."

"While you are doing that, I will check with Detective Rawlins to see what he has learned about Paul Lakefield's whereabouts," volunteered Timothy, wishing to make some contribution to the investigation.

"Well I have my work cut out for me," said Raymond. "Trying to mount a defense for Suzanne."

The three went their separate ways to carry out their self-appointed tasks. None of them confident that anything would be accomplished through their efforts but unable to stand by without trying something.

30

As expected, Katherine was the only individual at the estate when Melissa arrived. Having been friends for years, Melissa was surprised the woman had never mentioned her married name. Of course, if Paul Lakefield was the type of character they believed him to be, marriage to him, even though short-lived, was not the sort of thing one tended to spread around. It was in her past. No doubt where she had hoped it would remain.

"Hi Katherine, how are you?" Mel began. "When do you leave for your trip?"

"Tonight, actually," the woman replied. "I am looking forward to getting away. What can I do for you, Mel?"

"I was wondering if I could ask you a few questions?"

"What about?" asked the woman, her manner defensive.

Choosing her words cautiously, Melissa continued, "It seems Suzanne was involved with a Paul Lakefield, who worked at the agency. We have reason to believe he was the person embezzling the money from the company and, quite possibly, was also responsible for murdering Mark Dunn."

"So. What does that have to do with me?" Melissa surmised, from Katherine's tone, that the query was simply a formality.

"Detective Rawlins is having some difficulty locating the gentleman. Donald happened to mention a friend of his who addressed you by the same name. As Lakefield is an uncommon name we wondered if perhaps you knew the man?"

"Do you mean in the biblical sense? A person's past is a hard thing to bury, isn't it. One way, or another, it always haunts you. Yes, I knew the man. He was my husband for a very short period of time. Long enough for me to get pregnant. When I refused to have an abortion, he introduced his fists to my face and other parts of my anatomy. Following my exposure to the darker side of his personality, I left him and came here.

"He found out where I went and tracked me down. We are legally divorced and he was instructed to stay away from me and Cody. But it would take more than a court order to stop Paul. He threatened to harm my son if I refused to ask Mrs. Carson to give him a job at the agency, so I did. I lied and said he was my brother. She hired him on my recommendation. He is a despicable human being, but a fine artist."

"I was wondering why Judith would hire someone like him. She was usually so careful to weed out his type."

"She would have, had it not been for me. I think he knew that."

"Does Cody know Paul is his father?"

"No, I told him his father died in an automobile accident. As long as I do what Paul tells me to, he promised he would keep his identity a secret."

"Exactly how much hold does Paul have on you?"

"What do you mean?"

"Could he have forced you to poison Judith?"

"God, no. What type of person do you think I am? I loved Judith. None of Paul's threats could have made me harm one hair on her head. I would have killed him, rather than help him do anything so vile.

"Besides, I thought the police had proof that Suzanne was responsible for her mother's death."

"That is their guess but I think they are mistaken. Suzanne is many things. I just don't happen to believe murderer is one of them.

"By the way, I understand, from Suzanne, that you knew of her affair with Paul and used your knowledge to blackmail her into keeping you on here."

"Yes, that is true. I am not proud of what I did but it was necessary. She was planning to fire me, after her mother passed away. As I knew she would. We have never got along very well. I need this job, Mel and I am damn good at it. Suzanne had no complaints about my work. She just doesn't like me very much. I think, if the truth be known, she was jealous of the close relationship I enjoyed with Judith. I advised her that I knew of their affair and would expose her were she to fire me. Not the nicest way to keep a job, but extremely effective."

"I can understand your desperation. You have your son to consider. Suzanne admitted that herself. Of course, if she had fired you, you could have grieved it on the basis of unjust dismissal."

"I know, but my way was quicker."

"I don't doubt that." Mel could not help but chuckle. "Besides coming here to talk with you, I was hoping I could look around. Maybe discover something the police missed. Some clue which proves Suzanne's claim of innocence."

"You will get no objection from me. I don't think you will find anything though. The police were quite thorough."

Not thorough enough to have found the needle and syringe, Mel thought to herself. But then, she considered, perhaps the reason they did not find the articles was that they were not placed in Suzanne's closet until after the police had conducted their search. But why? If the person who had poisoned Judith wanted to frame Suzanne, why wait before planting the incriminating evidence?

One answer came to mind. Because the individual who framed Suzanne did not, initially, have the syringe in their possession. If Paul Lakefield was somehow involved in Judith's murder, he may have been the one who doctored the vitamin pills, thus being the one in possession of the equipment. Planting the evidence in Suzanne's room may have been an afterthought.

Melissa checked the areas extensively which she had missed on her previous visit. She found nothing. The only thing remotely of interest was the evidence of Connie's move to the guest room down the hall. Melissa knew about the woman's affairs but was under the impression that Donald chose to ignore his wife's indiscretions. Apparently, he chose to ignore them no longer.

Melissa was disappointed but had to admit her search was fruitless. The more she hunted, the more frustrated she became. She was accomplishing nothing.

I may as well return to the office for all I am getting done here, she decided.

Saying her good-byes to Katherine, Melissa departed.

As she drove around the loop of the driveway she noticed the door to Anna's cottage ajar. That is odd, she thought. They must have been in a hurry and neglected to close it tightly when they left. I had better stop and pull it to.

Melissa realized, as she got out of the car to do so, that she had never, in all the years she had visited the estate, seen the inside of the cottage.

It was a lovely building with the appearance of one from a fairy tale. Melissa remembered referring to the cottage, in that same way, as a child. During her walks with her aunt over the grounds, she had created an image in her mind of how the interior of the cottage would look. She wondered how close the real thing would come to her make believe picture.

Yielding to temptation—after all, the door was open, so she could hardly be accused of breaking and entering— Melissa opened the door.

The interior of the cottage was as exquisite as she had imagined, all these years. There were two bedrooms, a kitchen, dining room, living room and bath. Although the structure was relatively small, it would be comfortable for two people.

Melissa noticed the pictures of Anna and Carmelita, posing with members of their family, displayed around the living area. Scanning the photos, one in particular caught Mel's eye. It was a typical family scene of man, woman and child. But, something was wrong. She recognized the woman as Anna: the child she was holding obviously Carmelita. The man Melissa knew as well. She had seen numerous pictures of him before. But, he did not belong in this family scene. Anna belonged, Carmelita belonged, but what was Uncle Howard doing in this photo.

Reality dawned on the startled woman when her field of vision drifted to Carmelita's graduation picture on the mantle. The resemblance was uncanny. Why had she not noticed it before? She could not deny the truth revealed in the photo. Howard Carson had been Carmelita's natural father.

What does this mean? Melissa's troubled psyche pondered the significance of the revelation. Had Judith been aware of the connection between her husband and their maid? The affair must have taken place shortly after Anna began working for the Carsons.

Had her foot not slipped on the paper, Mel never would have noticed it lying on the floor, or bent to pick it up, thinking she must have knocked it off the mantel. The numbers written on the paper looked familiar. One was very familiar. It was the phone number of the Sunset View Inn. What reason would either Anna or Carmelita have to call the inn where Melissa had been staying?

The other digits were less recognizable, though Melissa knew the combination from somewhere. Grabbing the book located under the table phone she checked her suspicions. She was right. It was the number for the direct line into the agency's creative department.

Suddenly, everything became unmistakably clear. Melissa also knew that to remain in her present location was courting disaster. "Oh my God!" she exclaimed. "I have got to get out of here."

"No," said a voice behind her. "I don't think you are going anywhere, Melissa." The voice was Carmelita's. Melissa turned to face the younger woman and was aghast at the hatred apparent on her friend's countenance. Her facial appearance was not as frightening, however, as the rather ugly gun she was holding in her right hand. A gun she gave indication of knowing how to use, should Melissa give her any provocation to do so. "You had no business coming here, Mel. You should have stayed out of this. Suzanne is in jail where she belongs. Everything is as it should be. Why did you have to meddle?"

"It was you. You poisoned Judith. Why Carmelita? Why did you want Judith dead?"

"Because I wanted the agency. Mother told me that my father promised it would be mine. It was payment for her silence about their affair. And me. He said he would look after my future. That future included ownership of the agency. Don't you see? He promised it to me."

"But you didn't inherit the company."

"Don't you think I know that? You did. You, who knows nothing about running a business. And what did I get. Money. Unfortunately, that is not good enough. I want more, much more and I intend to have it."

"So, where do we go from here? Do you plan on killing me too?"

"I am sorry, Melissa. But it can't be helped. You are in my way. As a rule, I am opposed to violence. However, as Paul explained to me, there are times when it is the only workable solution. With Judith gone, Suzanne in jail for her murder and Paul taking care of Donald, you are the only remaining obstacle. You see, I really have no choice. You must see that."

The woman was deranged. That Melissa could plainly see. Her only way to escape the outcome Carmelita had planned for her was to keep the woman talking. As it was unlikely, after all that had transpired, that the woman could be convinced to let Mel go free, the best she could accomplish was to postpone the event long enough to hope someone came to her rescue. But who? The only person available was Katherine who would never realize what was taking place at the cottage, located some distance from the main house.

"Did you know about Suzanne's affair with Paul?"

"Of course. It was an integral part of our plan. One I suggested, I might add. Brilliant, eh? How else could he have got a copy of the key to the accounting department."

"How can Paul 'look after' Donald, when he has been placed under arrest?" Melissa knew her questions were a bit disjointed, but it was difficult to be totally coherent when one was terrified. She also knew that Paul Lakefield was still at large. She was hoping, however, to make Carmelita fall for the ruse. If she believed her colleague was in custody, the girl may acknowledge the wisdom of turning herself in, before further lives were endangered. Not a guaranteed reaction, but one worth challenging.

"I'm afraid you are mistaken. Paul escaped Detective Rawlins. He is, as we speak, placing a bomb under Donald's car. Bombs are, he told me, an extremely effective means of disposing of obstacles."

"For someone who professes an abhorrence of violence, you seem to be able to readily accept it, when it suits you to do so."

"As I said, there are times when it is the only way to eliminate a problem speedily."

"Paul will not elude Detective Rawlins forever. Mike is a determined man. He will capture your friend. It is just a matter of time."

"Even if he does, that really doesn't affect me. No one knows of our connection. Paul isn't the type to talk. I'll be free and clear. With you and Donald out of the way, the company will be mine."

"No, I don't think so, Carmelita. The game is over. Put down the gun." Carmelita recognized the voice. No, she thought, it isn't possible. She had killed the woman herself. She knew she had put enough arsenic in the warm milk. Judith could not still be alive.

"No," she screamed, as she turned to face the woman whom she had attempted to murder. "It can't be. I killed you."

"Afraid not, my dear. Although I will admit, you gave it one hell of a try."

Judith was not alone. Detective Rawlins was with her, as was Timothy. "Miss Gonzales, put down the gun," instructed the detective. Carmelita, realizing all her hopes were vanquished, turned the weapon on herself. Her movements were purposeful and rapid. However, Mel was quicker, stopping the girl's hand before she had time to pull the trigger.

31

It was finally over. With this realization came an over-whelming sense of relief. Paul Lakefield was dead. Killed in a crossfire with police, while attempting to escape capture. Fortunately, Carmelita had been mistaken when she presumed the man would not talk. He had spoken her name as his life was ebbing away. Had it not been for his final words, Rawlins and the others may have arrived too late to save Melissa.

Anna was devastated by Carmelita's arrest. She knew she had been wrong to give her daughter the misguided hope that she would inherit the company, upon Judith's death. Anna so wanted this to happen, she had believed it would. Somewhere, along the way, she had transformed a wish into reality.

Convincing herself and her daughter that it was a natural progression of events.

"Were you aware of Uncle Howard's affair with Anna?" Melissa asked her aunt.

"I had my suspicions but we never discussed it. You see, not long after we moved here, Howard and I were experiencing some trouble in our marriage. Financial difficulties, brought on by his excessive and unwise spending. I did not feel particularly affectionate toward your uncle during that period. He went to Anna for consolation. Solace she readily provided.

"Though I was fairly certain there was something between them, I was brought up to believe that, once a person got married, it was for keeps. Bearing that in mind, I stuck it out.

"Needless to say, our marriage weathered that storm and many others. To my knowledge, that was the only time Howard ever cheated on me."

"Why didn't you fire Anna, if you suspected their involvement?" Melissa was confused over her aunt's reaction to her husband's affair.

"Why should I? She was a good worker. The problem existed between Howard and myself. Anna was simply a scapegoat for our troubles. It was hardly fair to blame her for my husband's indiscretions."

"You are a lot more understanding than I would have been," announced Mel.

"Not really. I considered leaving him. Went so far as to pack my bags. But, at the last minute, decided it was in my best interests to stay. To this day, I have never regretted that decision."

"But why provide for Anna and her daughter so handsomely in your will?"

"Because, it was the right thing to do. Carmelita was Howard's daughter, too. She deserved the same advantages as his other children. It is unfortunate that things turned out the way they did."

"Yes. Although, it is doubtful if it could have been prevented."

"I don't know," said Judith. "It seems to me these things can always be prevented."

The door to the mansion opened and Judith's children entered. Raymond had forewarned them of Judith's continued existence and how they had carried out the ruse, therefore they were prepared. Although they were not surprised by the sight of her, pleased they definitely were.

"Mother," greeted Donald. "It is so good to see you."

"And you, my dear." Melissa had told her aunt of the startling transformation she had noticed in Donald and, more recently, Suzanne. Changes which were apparent in the degree of genuine emotion they displayed upon seeing their mother.

"That was quite an ingenious plot you devised. How did you get the hospital and the ambulance personnel to go along?"

"Through the efforts of Dr. Adams. He explained to the administration the circumstances and they agreed to go along. You two saved us some trouble, by not requesting to see my remains. That would have proved a bit dicey.

"Fooling the police was the hardest part. We had to make sure they believed I was dead. That wasn't easy. It's a good thing the coroner is a good friend of mine. Falsifying autopsy results is a serious offense. He was taking quite a risk by helping us."

"I can't believe you actually thought we wanted you dead. We have been very wrong," said Suzanne. "I see that now. So much of what you and Father tried to teach us we rebelled against. Spending a short time in jail made me realize that I really am no better than anyone else. And, all the money in the world, cannot keep bad things from happening."

"Where is Raymond?" asked Judith, wishing to thank the young man who had played such an integral part in their plan.

"Right here, Ma'am." The lawyer approached the woman for a well-deserved hug. "You look to be in fine form."

"That I am."

"Mother, where is your wheelchair?" asked Donald, realizing his mother was walking unassisted.

"I don't need it. My legs are much stronger now. That is not to say I will not need it again. But, for now, I am free."

"Where have you been all this time?" Suzanne asked.

"I went on the cruise, as planned. Dr. Adams replaced Melissa as my traveling companion. By the way, in future I will be addressed as Mrs. Adams."

"Congratulations," offered Raymond. "We will have to plan a double ceremony. Suzanne has agreed to marry me, as well."

"Well, it's about time my daughter came to her senses," laughed Judith.

"Ain't that the truth," acknowledged Donald. "It is rather ironic, you know."

"What is?" asked his sister.

"Here I am getting divorced and the two women in my family are getting married."

"I'm sorry, Son."

"Don't be. It is something I should have done years ago."

"Maybe it is for the best."

"I believe so, Mother." Donald thought it wise to mention his new love interest at a later time.

"How is the agency?"

Melissa started to summarize the difficulties which had transpired during the woman's absence.

"That's right. There was a small problem just before I went away. I never did find out who was behind it. Just as I started to check it out, my health got worse. It was my intention to get back to Timothy about it but I simply forgot. Not like me. But, I guess, I was hardly myself at the time."

"Well, everything is fine. Now that you are back," said Mel. She saw no need to mention Suzanne's affair with Paul and the resultant cover-up of his actions.

"I take it you did not totally enjoy your stint in the advertising business."

"You could say that. Give me a cardiac arrest any day. At least I know what to do with that type of crisis."

"Don't let her fool you," said Timothy. "She did just fine.

As if she were born to it. You should have seen the way she handled Seymour Allen."

"Sounds as though we could use her services to head up our public relations department," suggested Judith.

"I think that is an excellent idea. That way we can keep her around," agreed Timothy.

"You would like me to stay around?" asked Mel.

"Yes, Ms. Sommers, I would like that very much."

"Sounds to me as though we may have to plan for a larger ceremony," noted Raymond.

"You may just have to do that," said Timothy.

"What about you, Mother? Are you resuming your responsibilities at the agency?" asked Donald.

"No, my dear boy, you will be taking over the role of general manager. I expect you will do a fine job, with some guidance from Timothy."

"I will try my best." Donald was overwhelmed by the news of his appointment.

"I must apologize to you all for the trouble and heartache my disappearance caused. However, it was the only way I could think of to find out who was trying to poison me. It was cruel and, for that, I am deeply sorry."

"Let's talk no more about it. You are back, safe and sound, where you belong." Everyone nodded affirmatively to Donald's statement.

"Just think, Mother, of all the good that came out of this. Our relationship will be so much stronger now. Perhaps we can even start to act like a family again." Suzanne's words clearly displayed the astounding change in her, since her temporary incarceration.

"Wouldn't that be nice?" agreed Judith. "And what about you, Suzanne? Are you planning to resume your duties at Carson Agency?"

"No, Mother. I realize, now, advertising is not for me. Most of my time will be spent trying to be a good wife to Raymond and seeking out a career more suited to my personality and abilities.

"First and foremost, I have to mend some fences. Had it not been for my poor choice of associates, I never would have found myself in this situation, to begin with. Perhaps it is time to develop some new friendships."

Judith was aware of Suzanne's affair with Paul Lakefield and the fact that she had withheld what she knew of his activities. That was, however, in the past. She did not plan to bring the subject up, unless her daughter mentioned it.

After all, everyone makes mistakes. Even Judith had made her share. The fact that Suzanne had apparently learned from hers was the important thing.

Judith had been wrong to think her children would, consciously, do her harm. Suzanne was not the only one intent on mending fences. She had a few of her own which needed repair.

Judith knew that life would now be better. She planned to see to that, personally.